MR. ADAM

BOOKS BY PAT FRANK

An Affair of State
Alas, Babylon
Forbidden Area
Hold Back the Night
Mr. Adam

MR. ADAM

A Novel

PAT FRANK

HARPER PERENNIAL

NEW YORK • LONDON • TORONTO • SYDNEY • NEW DELHI • AUCKLAND

HARPER ● PERENNIAL

HarperCollins books may be purchased for educational, business, or sales promotional use. For information please email the Special Markets Department at SPsales@harpercollins.com.

Library of Congress Cataloging-in-Publication Data has been applied for.

ISBN 978-0-06-242176-0

16 17 18 19 20 OV/RRD 10 9 8 7 6 5 4 3 2 1

for
Doris and Mont

MR. ADAM

CHAPTER 1

I suppose it is up to me to tell the story in its entirety, because I broke it in the first place, and I lived with it from then on, and I grew to know Mr. Adam. My name is Stephen Decatur Smith, and before I got involved in the most important story in the world I was a feature writer on the New York staff of AP. I specialized in ship launchings, and sports spectacles, and indignation sprees at Town Hall, and the like. I inhabit the ground floor of a brownstone house on West Tenth Street. I am still married, which is a surprise to me.

I got a break on the story strictly by accident, which is of course the way you get most big beats. Most guys who win the Pulitzer Prize are also lucky at shooting craps.

It started on the night I covered the Zionist rally in the Garden. When the last resolution had been unanimously adopted I went hurtling out of the Garden, bound for Toots Shor's. I never got there, because of my trick knee, and the fat lady. When the fat lady loomed up at the Eighth Avenue entrance I tried some fast evasive action and my trick knee went out on me. If it had not been for that medium tank of a woman the world would not have known for weeks, or perhaps several months, what had happened to it.

I let out a yell, and collapsed against the building, and the fat lady's mouth flew open, and she put on a burst of speed and got out of there. I knew she thought I was having a fit.

Right across the street from the Garden is Polyclinic Hospital, strategically situated for hockey, rodeo, wrestling, and prize-fight casualties. Some of the very best surgeons in town are on the staff there. They like it, because they never know what will come into the Emergency Room next. As Dr. Thompson says, "It's like an evac hospital plus a maternity ward."

It was Thompson I saw after I'd hobbled across the street. He's a friendly elephant of a man with brown, stubby hands. I'd known him in Italy, during the Gothic Line campaign, when he was running the station hospital outside Florence. I remember watching him with wonder as he worked among the wounded, using those great, powerful hands on the mud-caked doughs as tenderly as a woman touching an infant's face.

He went to work with those hands on my knee, and in a moment there was one short, sharp pain, and then my knee was good again, as I knew it would be. "It'll jump out," he warned, "whenever you try any brokenfield running in traffic."

"I know," I said. "Come on down to Shor's and hoist a couple."

"Can't," Thompson said. "I've got a mystery. The board had a meeting today, and they discovered a mystery, and they delegated me to find out why."

"What's the mystery?" I asked.

Thompson hesitated a moment. Then he said: "I'll brief you on it. But it's not for publication. Not yet. You see, it's the no reservations in the maternity ward."

"No reservations. That's strange."

"Very. There's never been less hospital space, compared to the population, than in the last few years, and it has actually been getting worse since the war ended. You see, the increase in the birth rate has been fantastic. You'd think everybody in the United States had settled on one occupation and hobby, and that was producing babies. Why, we've been getting reservations for our maternity ward as long as eight months in advance."

"How can they be sure?" I asked.

"They cannot. But they just speculate. That's the Broadway crowd for you." Thompson examined the big loose-leaf ledger on his desk. "Then suddenly," he said, "nothing at all!"

"You don't mean," I suggested, "that people have quit having babies?"

"All I know for certain," said Thompson, "is that people have quit making reservations to have their babies in Polyclinic Hospital, as of June 22."

I looked at the ledger. There were twenty names, addresses, telephone numbers, names of attending physicians, and amounts of deposit listed for every day in May, and every day in June, until June 22. Then, as he said, nothing at all.

I said, my finger on June 11: "What do you know, Dotty Fair's going to be a mamma! Just for fun, I think I'll scoop Winchell."

"Now look," said Thompson, "this is serious."

"Ridiculous!" I said. "Preposterous! Imagine an institution like Polyclinic spinning in a tizzy because people have decided not to make reservations five months ahead! Hospitals are just money-grubbing, capitalistic corporations, as I've always suspected. The truth is that people have just got damned sick and tired of kowtowing to those sacred, omnipotent institutions, the hospitals, and have decided to have their babies at home. And I might remind you that up until about a century ago all babies were born at home."

Thompson scratched his nose, and said: "Now if a lot of new hospitals had been built, or if we'd had a dysentery epidemic, and a lot of kids had been killed, it would be explainable. But I tell you, Stephen, nowadays they don't wait until the honeymoon is over to call the hospital."

I said, soothingly, "I'll come back tomorrow, and you'll find it's been all a mistake, and that some file clerk, fresh out of the WACS, has been bucking all the reservations to the next highest echelon."

I decided not to go to Shor's. When you get to Shor's there are a lot of other newspapermen there and they drink, and talk, and sometimes one of them tells about a story he is going to write for the Sunday section, and then he reads it in another paper on Saturday. I took the Eighth Avenue subway, and walked into our apartment at midnight.

The fire logs were thin, bigger at the ends than in the middle, and in the middle only the blue flame of the dying fire spurted. Marge was on the davenport, asleep, with her long legs crossed and her hands folded across her stomach, and the New York *Post* shielding her face from the light. The headlines told of fighting in Palestine, China, Burma, and Syria, which is about par for peacetime, but the news didn't bother me, because Marge was more interesting.

I tiptoed across the room and leaned over to kiss her hair, and she pulled the paper aside and winked at me, and I knew she wasn't sleeping and kissed her on the mouth instead. I'm the old-fashioned monogamous species of man who loves his wife.

"What's the matter," she said, "coming right home like this?"

"A moment without you," I explained, "is a moment wasted."

"You're just feeling lustful," she said, "or you would be in a pub." She looked up at me, speculating. It's amazing, what a woman can find out about a man in four years. "No," she decided, "it's not that. You want to tell me about a story."

"Uh-huh," I admitted, and I told her about Dr. Thompson and the hospital.

"I think," she said when I'd finished, "that it's time we had a baby. The war's over, the world is settling down, there's space in the hospitals, and it is time we started building a family. Besides, you're not getting any younger."

"I'm only thirty-eight!"

"That's practically middle-aged. Sometimes I think we should have had a baby right away."

"Come on," I said, "what do you think is wrong at Polyclinic?"

"Nothing at all," Marge said, "except all my friends have been going to Episcopal. I think I'll go to Episcopal. I want a big room, with a radio, and I'll want my own nurse for at least the first three days. Weren't we dopes not to subscribe to group hospitalization?"

"Maybe you have forgotten," I suggested with what I considered to be irony, "that it takes two to make a baby."

She kissed me again. "Darling," she said, "I am so glad you came home early tonight."

During the next week there was a blizzard in New England, La Guardia turned down the job of military governor of Germany, and prime ministers, jobless kings, and jobless generals arrived every day by plane from Europe. They all had to be interviewed, and I had forgotten about Dr. Thompson and his mystery.

I forgot, that is, until one day I found myself staring up at Episcopal Hospital, and I recalled that Marge preferred Episcopal, and just on a hunch I went inside.

I was inquiring, I told the red-headed girl in the office, about the possibility of reserving a room in the maternity section, say about June 20. The girl dipped into a filing cabinet. She came back to the counter, shook her head, and smiled. "Too bad," she said. "We're booked solid for June 20. Now if it was just two days later—"

"You mean," I said, feeling my stomach knot up inside me, "that you have plenty of space for the twenty-second?"

"For the twenty-second," she said, "we don't have a single reservation. As a matter of fact, we don't have any at all beyond June

21." The redhead frowned. "That *is* peculiar," she said. "That is *very* peculiar. Funny I didn't notice it before."

"Thank you very much," I said, and I left, and noticed as I walked out into the snow that she was telephoning, and that the frown had not gone from her face.

I went to the AP office and called five other hospitals. Then I walked into J.C. Pogey's inner sanctum, unannounced. I certainly was shaken, and I suppose I must have been white with fright and foreboding, because when J.C. saw me he said: "For Christ's sake what's the matter?"

I fell into the leather chair by his desk, and tried to light a cigarette. I couldn't make my hands behave, and J.C. held a match for me. "It may be the most frightful thing!" I said. "The most frightful thing!"

"What?"

"No babies. No babies after June 21."

J.C. Pogey is a very old, and patient, and infinitely wise man who has been the New York manager since, it is believed, the Administration of Taft. In that time all the most startling events of history have flowed through his ancient and delicate fingers, so what must have appeared to him as the spectacle of a reporter going wacky could not be expected to move him overmuch. He said, gently, "All right, Steve, take it easy and tell me the tale."

I started with my knee, and went through the whole chronology. When I had finished he did not speak for a time, but rubbed his bald head behind the ears with his thin thumbs—a sort of manual method he employed to induce rapid cerebration.

Finally he said: "It may be, of course, the most terrible and certainly the most important story since the Creation. We must make the most thorough check, and yet we must not reveal what we're after, or do anything that will bring premature publication. It may be simply an extraordinary coincidence—but I'm afraid not."

"That's pretty pessimistic," I said.

J.C. swung his high-backed chair until it faced the window, and he looked out upon the spires of the city, soft gold in the winter sun, and it seemed that he looked through and beyond. "If I were God," he said, "and I were forced to pick a time to deprive the human race of the magic power of fertility and creation, I think that time would be now."

We decided that I should check the story, as far as possible, by telephone. We didn't want to send any more queries or cables than necessary, because when you start sending queries you get a lot of other people excited, and the story is likely to get beyond your control.

I armed myself with telephone directories for twenty big cities. I started by calling a hospital in Boston. I didn't say it was the AP calling. I just said I was a prospective father. The Boston hospital was booked up for June 21, like those in New York, but I was somewhat relieved when they said they had a few reservations for the last week in June.

"I don't think that is important," J.C. warned. "I think you'll find it is just a miscalculation by some Boston doctor. That's bound to happen."

I called Rochester, Philadelphia, Miami, and New Orleans, and then desperately swung west to San Francisco. The situation was identical. I called Chicago, St. Louis, and Omaha, and then tried some small towns in the South. So far as I could discover, our July birth rate was going to be zero.

"Maybe it's only in the United States," I suggested.

"Try Montreal and Mexico City and B.A. and Rio," J.C. ordered.

I found I was hungry, and that it was night, and we sent out for sandwiches and coffee, and I began combing the Western Hemisphere. Things didn't change.

"This isn't proving anything," I said at midnight. "Maybe there isn't any shortage of hospital space. The only people who really know about this are the obstetricians."

"All right," said J.C., "call some obstetricians." I knew, by the way he said it, that his mind was set. A night fog had rolled over the city, and a Europe-bound liner was moaning its way toward the sea. He kept staring out into the night as if he expected to see something.

I only knew one obstetrician, Maria Ostenheimer, a friend of Marge who lives around the corner on Fifth Avenue. While I dialed her number, I noticed that J.C. was scribbling on an outgoing message form.

Dr. Ostenheimer was awake, and by the noise, she was having a party. I said, "Maria, I've got something serious, and very confidential to ask you."

"Marge was over here, and she left a half-hour ago," Dr. Ostenheimer said. "She came over here alone, and she left alone, and I think you're a pig to even suspect . . ."

"No! No! No! This is nothing like that," I interrupted. "This is strictly business, and damn vital business."

"If you're going to have a baby," she said, "it'll be both a relief and a surprise, because nobody else is having babies." Her voice was just a bit hysterical, I thought.

"That's what I called about," I said, "this business of no babies."

There was a pause, and I knew she had shut the door to her rumpus room, because the party noises ceased. "What do you know about it?" she asked.

"I know that the hospitals aren't getting reservations in the maternity wards after June 21. That's not only here, but all over the country, all over other countries too."

There was no sound from the other end of the phone, and I thought for a moment that Maria might have fainted. But then she said, in a hushed, tense voice: "Stephen, at first I thought it was me. At first I thought somebody was spreading vicious lies about my work, and that I was being secretly blackballed. You know I've got a big practice, Stephen, and then suddenly, a few months ago, no new patients came. I start in the beginning with prenatal care, you know, Stephen."

"You only accept a limited number of patients each month, but that quota is always filled, right?"

"That's right. Well, it's awfully hard, going to a colleague and announcing that you're not getting any new patients, and I kept quiet until a few days ago, and then Dr. Blandy—he's got a big practice in Westchester—dropped in to see me, and I felt that the same thing was worrying him, and all of a sudden he told me, and I told him that the same thing had happened to me. We've talked to six others—I suppose together they're the top obstetricians in Manhattan—and we're having a meeting next week to investigate."

"You keep it quiet," I said, thinking of the story, although when I look back on it now a news beat seems very small potatoes, and indeed almost irrelevant. "You keep quiet about this, but I'll want to see you about it later."

I hung up, and turned to J.C. "I think," I said, "that the world has had it!"

"Perhaps not the whole world," said J.C. "Perhaps only the Western Hemisphere." He handed me the message form. It read:

URGENT PRESS FYI ONLY FYI ONLY USING UTMOST DISCRETION ASCERTAIN WHETHER ANY SUDDEN DROP BIRTHRATE EXPECTED LOCALLY JUNE OR JULY STOP REPLY PERSONALLY URGENTEST POGEY

"We'll send this immediately," he said, "to Pat Morin in Paris, and Boots Norgaard in Rome, and Frank O'Brien in Istanbul, and Goldberg in Budapest, and Eddy Gilmore in Moscow. And of course to the London Bureau."

"They'll think you're nuts," I said.

"They will until they've checked up," said J.C. "Then they'll be frightened, just as you are, and just as I am. We won't get answers to these queries until tomorrow, so you go on home to that blonde wife of yours, and get plenty of sleep, because I do not believe you will be sleeping very much for a week or so."

One of our best spies told me, once, that there were only two kinds of wives—those to whom you told nothing, and those to whom you told everything. I tell Marge everything, but on this night I kept my mouth shut, because I knew if we started talking about it I'd never get any sleep. Besides, I was afraid. I didn't know how she'd react if I told her it didn't appear likely that we'd ever have any babies. I felt desolate, and empty inside. I consumed a good deal of rye, straight, before I slept.

In the morning Marge brought coffee to bed, which was unusual, and she said: "Stephen, you're not sick, are you?"

"No. I've got to get up. I've got to go to the office early."

"Stephen, what's the trouble?"

"Nothing," I said, and put the covers over my head and crawled into the middle of "Smith Field." We have the most enormous double bed in New York, built for lazy living. It's surrounded by a shelf, and gadgets. On one side we have a radio, and a bookcase, and on the other a little refrigerator and bar. Our friends say our bed is decadent, and indecent, but we like it, and call it Smith Field.

"There's no use hiding," said Marge. "Come out from under there. You've either been gambling, or there's been trouble at the office, or you're sick. Something really bad has happened. I know."

"It's just that I'm a little hung over," I lied.

"Is it that hospital business you talked about last week?"

I didn't reply, but I knew that she knew. "I don't know why," Marge said, "but I've been worrying about it."

"Nothing is certain, yet," I said. When I left the house I kissed her with what I thought was reassurance. But I had never before seen

Marge's face so strained, and her eyes so dull, and lacking of life. On the way uptown it seemed that I stood apart and alone from all the others on the streets and in the subway. The bustle of New York going to work on a weekday morning seemed altogether futile and without meaning.

J.C. had a little stack of teletype messages on his desk, and I knew the verdict before I read them, simply by the set of his shoulders, and by his silence.

The answers were all the same. So far as anyone could determine, no more children would be born after the last week in June. In Paris and London, very secret official investigations had already been started.

"We've got answers," said J.C., "from everywhere except Moscow," but even as he spoke an office boy brought in another incoming teletype. It was from the Moscow Bureau. It read:

```
URGENT PRESS ASSOCIATED NEW YORK PROPOGEY
SOVIET GOVERNMENT PERTURBEDEST MY INQUIRIES
STOP MY EXPULSION THREATENED PROATTEMPTING
PENETRATE STATE SECRETS STOP HOWEVER YOUR
HUNCH CORRECT GILMORE
```

"That's enough for me," said J.C.

"It seems to me," I said, "that the whole world knows about this thing, and is trying to keep it a secret."

"I don't blame the whole world," said J.C. "The whole world is like a man who knows he has cancer, but won't admit it, even to himself. However, it has to break some time, and as long as it has to break, the AP might as well break it."

"We'll have to put the Washington Bureau on it, for official statements, and the American Medical Association. But—why?"

"That's it—why?"

"There must be a scientific reason."

J.C. put the worn serge of his elbows on his desk and massaged his head behind his ears. "All night," he said, "I kept thinking of something General Farrell said after he witnessed the first atomic bomb explosion in New Mexico. He said, if I remember the words correctly, that the explosion 'warned of doomsday and made us feel that we puny things were blasphemous to dare tamper with the forces heretofore reserved to the Almighty.'"

I recalled a kindred phrase, after Hiroshima was atomized, about civilization now having the power to commit suicide at will. I thought about it, and I thought of the Mississippi disaster, and the thing began to come clear to me, and I yelled: "When was it that Mississippi blew up? Wasn't it in September?"

J.C. straightened. "That's it, of course!" he said. "The Mississippi explosion was September the twenty-first. Nine months to the day! Nine months to the very day!"

CHAPTER 2

You will remember that on September 21 the great new nuclear fission plants at Bohrville, Mississippi—a city erected in the center of the state and named after one of the famous atomic physicists—disintegrated in an explosion that made Nagasaki and Hiroshima mere cap pistols by comparison.

Not only did Bohrville disintegrate but most of Mississippi went along with it. The blinding glare of the Bohrville disaster was seen as far north as Chicago, and across the Gulf of Mexico. St. Louis felt it as an earthshock, while the heat was dangerous in New Orleans.

What caused the explosion no man knew, for naturally there were no survivors. But it was known in Washington that the Bohrville plants were producing U-235, Plutonium, and even rarer and more violently radioactive substances in quantities that had been impossible in the plants at Oak Ridge, Tennessee, and Hanford, Washington.

The effects of the explosion upon the world were profound, and not all of them could be classed as evil. For one thing the United

States stopped making atomic bombs, and the other nations showed no desire to begin where we left off. Molotov issued a statement blaming the explosion on the greedy capitalistic system, and assured the Russians that there were no nuclear fission plants within the borders of the Soviet Union. In the Argentine, certain pro-Fascist scientists suddenly ceased their private experiments, and began to take up botany and ichthyology.

The United Nations had no trouble pledging its members to outlaw the atom as a weapon of war, but of course small wars kept going on, around the world.

Besides, nobody really missed Mississippi. The explosion eliminated Bilbo and Rankin, and anyway Mississippi was the most backward of states. People felt that if any one of the forty-eight states had to be sacrificed, it was just as well that it happened to Mississippi.

After the explosion I was assigned to interview the atomic physicists who lived in the New York area as to the probable cause, and the results. I remembered, now, that all the physicists had assured me that the explosion was only dangerous within a radius of a few hundred miles. But always I had had a disquieting feeling that there was something else they wished to say, but were afraid to say. It was as if there were something they were afraid to put into words, even to themselves.

Whenever I had asked about possible sterilization from Gamma rays, they'd clam up. Or they had pointed out, in words carefully picked and studied (for they knew they were talking for publication) that radioactive substances emitted Gamma rays "for only a comparatively short time." Then they'd lapse into the jargon of the physicist, and lead me into a dark scientific jungle where my pedestrian, layman's learning cast only a dim light.

Now I went to Professor Felix Pell, up at Columbia University. I went to Pell because, of all the surviving atomic physicists, he had talked least about the Mississippi disaster, although I had felt at the time that he could have told most.

Pell is a little man with narrow shoulders and uncertain legs, and you feel his body was constructed simply as a temporary support for his massive head. On his feet he is a caricature of a college professor, but in his own office, his shrunken body hidden behind an immense desk, he is imposing as a Supreme Court Justice posing for his first post-appointment picture.

Pell received me in his office. "I suppose," he suggested, "that you're still troubled about that business in Mississippi."

"Well, not exactly," I said. "I'm not troubled about Mississippi. Now I'm troubled about the world."

Professor Pell allowed himself to smile, but I had a feeling—reporters are always getting feelings or they wouldn't be reporters—that he was not completely at ease.

"It appears," I said, reaching into my pocket for a cigarette in my attempt to be completely casual, "that the Mississippi explosion sterilized the human race."

I will say this for Professor Pell. He was emotionally shockproof. "A most peculiar statement," he said. "I haven't heard anything about the human race being sterilized."

"That is because," I said, "you are not, at this stage in humanity's development, able to read tomorrow's newspapers."

"You are serious?"

"I certainly am. I am sterile, and you are sterile."

The professor's head twisted on the thin, wrinkled stem of his neck, and he peered up at me for a period of seconds. Then he dropped his eyes and said: "And what has this alleged sterilization got to do with the Mississippi catastrophe?"

"Since Mississippi blew up, no babies have been conceived anywhere on earth, so far as we can find out."

"That is hardly scientific proof."

I suddenly discovered that I hated Professor Pell. Up to this moment I had regarded him with a great deal of respect, and even awe, for was he not one of the superior beings who had, in the President's words, tapped the source from which the sun draws its power?

But of a sudden I hated him, and I knew that I would not be alone in my hate. I put my hands on his desk, and leaned over it until my face was close to his face. "Professor Pell," I said, "it may not be scientific proof, but it is pretty damn good circumstantial evidence." I fixed my eyes on his turkey-thin neck. "It is good enough evidence to hang a man," I continued. "It is good enough evidence to hang any man who even looked sideways at an atom."

I could see that I had shaken Pell loose from his equanimity. In this moment he was an old man, afraid for his life. "Please sit down," he said, "and tell me what you want of me, but I would rather not have my name connected with this."

"You didn't mind having your name at the top of the list when they were passing out credit for developing the bomb."

He nodded. "That is true," he said slowly. "That is perfectly true, and with the credit must go the blame. We have always known that this risk existed, and certainly at every stage in our research and production we took the most careful precautions to safeguard our personnel. But the risk was always there."

Pell touched a stapled sheaf of papers on the corner of his desk. I could read *Top Secret* on the first page. "Ever since the Mississippi explosion," he continued, "we have speculated on the possible harmful effects of unloosing such an unprecedented quantity of radioactive substances—along with obscure rays of which we know little—upon the earth. This is my analysis, which I was about to forward to the National Research Council."

"And what was your conclusion?" I asked.

"My conclusion," he said hesitantly, "was that such an explosion would send very penetrating radiations, encompassing the whole spectrum, around the world with the speed of light. Not only Gamma rays, and Alpha and Beta rays and particles, but their obscure variations. It was also my conclusion that these rays would prove harmful, but to what extent it was impossible to predict."

"Now we know," I said.

"Yes, indeed," Pell said, "now we know." Then he added: "Tell me, were women affected as well as men?"

"Of course the investigations aren't complete," I said. "A group of doctors has been making as many examinations as possible. But thus far they've found that all men are sterilized without exception, while few if any women were affected. The doctors say almost all women still ovulate, and the Fallopian tubes have not been damaged."

"The human body," said Pell, "is a strange business. There are chemistries of the body more mysterious than any problem in physics. Now I asked that question for a good reason. Men have always been more susceptible to certain rays than women. But all known harmful rays have affected both men and women. So the ray which did the damage must be one with which we are not as yet familiar."

"I don't see that it matters very much," I said.

"Well," said Pell, "it is an interesting aspect of the phenomenon, although its importance henceforth can only be classed as theoretical."

"Henceforth," I said, rising, "the importance of everything will only be theoretical." He was puzzling that one out as I left.

That night we began to move the story across our wires. The reactions, throughout the world, were immediate and fearful. I could trot out all the Hollywood adjectives, and run them into a sentence, two by two, like Noah's animals entering the Ark, and they would not begin to describe what started happening that night, and kept on happening.

J.C. Pogey, handling the story with no more flurry than if it were a national election, kept me at the rewrite desk until dawn. By that time, the story was not dissimilar to an election, for the whole world was split straight up the middle—those who believed it and those who didn't.

Strange little sidebar stories began to creep into the main trunk wires.

In Boston, an eminent churchman, hauled from his bed by the local press, denounced the whole thing as a vicious hoax. In Baltimore an equally eminent churchman said he'd been expecting it all along, and added that he wouldn't be at all surprised if the world didn't blow up within forty-eight hours.

In London, the King spoke over the BBC, and reassured the Empire that His Majesty's government was, and had been, well aware of the situation, was conducting an investigation, and was taking the necessary steps.

There were riots in Paris, but there are always riots in Paris.

Moscow cut itself off from the world.

The President urged the nation to be calm.

Up in Morningside Heights, a group of serious young women stoned the apartment house inhabited by Professor Pell.

Spontaneous rumors started simultaneously in Vienna, Budapest, Frankfurt am Main. Madrid and Berne said it was a plot on the part of Jewish scientists.

But it is best, perhaps, to describe what went on in my own particular household.

When I got home, just after the milkman but before the morning papers, Marge was curled up in one corner of Smith Field. I could tell, by the number of cigarette butts, that she had been up all night, undoubtedly listening to the news on the radio. The radio was still on, tuned to a Newark station, and giving out boogie-woogie.

I undressed, tossing my trousers and shirt across the back of a chair. I was examining myself in the full length mirror, wondering how a man who kept such irregular hours, and ate so erratically, could develop a definite belly, when the boogie-woogie faded, and a girl announcer said in the peculiar clipped sing-song which is currently the fashion among swing shift announcers:

"We are interrupting for another news flash. Washington—Surgeon General George Gail announced that he has called a congress of the nation's leading physicians and scientists early next week.

They will meet in the capital to plan national re-fertilization. Next you will hear that international wartime favorite, 'Lili Marlene,' and while I adjust the needle, let me remind you that this program comes to you through the courtesy of SILK E. RUB Furniture Polish, pronounced Silky Rub, the polish of Gracious Living."

In the background I could hear the opening bars of "Lili Marlene," and then a deep-voiced female quartet cut in with:

> *For all the news of sterilization*
> *Please keep tuned to this station.*

"Lili Marlene" swelled up, and I remembered the last time I had heard it, and the lyrics that went with it, while the Army trucks bound for the repple-depple in Naples rumbled by, and I began to sing the lyrics aloud:

> *Please, Mr. Truman, let the boys go home.*
> *We have conquered Naples, and we have captured*
> *Rome.*
> *We have licked the master race,*
> *Now all we want is shipping space.*
> *Oh, please, may we go home!*
> *Let the boys at home see Rome!*

Marge stirred, and inched across Smith Field until she reached the corner farthest away from me. "Damn you!" she grumbled sleepily. "Damn you!"

"I'm sorry, darling," I said. "Had to work all night. Big story."

Marge propped herself on her elbows and rubbed her eyes. "I'll say it was a big story," she exclaimed. "Oh, yes, it was the very biggest story—you eunuch, you!"

I didn't say anything, because it was the first time I had heard it put that way, and I was somewhat shocked, but I began to understand that the situation was complicated beyond anything either I or J.C. had imagined.

"You eunuch, you!" she repeated.

"Is that nice?" I inquired.

Marge sat up straight. She wore the red silk pajamas fashioned from the ammo chute I'd scrounged when the British paratroops jumped into Megara, Greece. You put a blonde into red pajamas, piped with white silken parachute cord, and ruffle her hair, and let indignant fire run out of her eyes, and you have something particularly lovable, if she is in the mood to be loved. She was not in that mood. She said: "You sleep on your own side of the field!"

"But darling," I protested, "is it my fault?"

"Of course it's your fault," she said. "At least it is your fault that we didn't start any children before it happened."

"Who was it," I asked, "who said the world wasn't a fit place to produce babies?"

"That was in forty-three," she retorted. "It wasn't, then."

"Is it my fault, entirely," I enquired, "that Mississippi blew up? Simply because Mississippi blew up, are we going to go through the remainder of our lives like distant and not-too-friendly cousins?"

"Stephen Decatur Smith," Marge said, "I know it sounds silly to you but I think it is a dirty trick on the part of the whole male population. For the rest of your lives you will be rabbiting around, smirking, all equipped with built-in contraceptives."

It didn't seem necessary to answer. I got into my own side of Smith Field. "Not being a woman, you could never completely understand," Marge went on. "Men will continue to live their lives. But to every woman, it will be as if she were already dead."

Later, I found that Marge's evaluation was accurate, and until the miracle of Mr. Adam, the feminine suicide rate rose considerably.

But generally, life continued on an astoundingly normal plane. The world ticked on, like a clock that would never be wound again, but which would continue to tell time and sound off the hours until it finally ran down.

Winter slipped into spring. There was the usual art fair in Washington Square. Young people in love held hands and planned plastic houses, including nurseries, in the blind confidence of love and youth. Radical plastic automobiles appeared, the United Nations reached agreement on the Hungarian-Slovak border, and a United States oil company succeeded in obtaining a ninety-nine-year lease on the new field in Iraq.

The front pages of the newspapers, of course, were devoted to little except stories on World Sterilization, or, as abbreviated by the tabloid headline writers, W.S. But so long as babies continued to be born, the whole thing seemed incredible and fantastic, and indeed it was denounced every day, officially, by experts such as Congressmen, Anglican Bishops, the President of the Chamber of Commerce, Dorothy Thompson, and three- and four-star generals.

But things began to get tense in June, and as the month slid by, apprehension increased. By this time, of course, the facts had been so well established, in every country and on every continent, including the interior of Africa and the Eskimos near the Pole, that there was no reason for hope—and yet hope persisted. On June 21 the *Daily News* ran a banner, "W.S. DAY TOMORROW!"

The world held its breath, prepared for the worst, and the worst happened.

For the remainder of the month, and indeed well into July, there were sporadic bursts of optimism as communities reported births, but all these, it developed, were the result of over-long periods of gestation.

False alarms were frequent, naturally, and we realized that they would continue for a generation or two. But for the most part, by autumn the world had composed itself to slow death, although the

President had allotted unlimited funds, and all science had been enlisted, for the N.R.P., or National Re-fertilization Project. The Sunday supplements began to speculate as to who would inherit the earth—the insects, or the fishes.

On the first anniversary of the Mississippi explosion I awoke at noon. Marge was sitting, cross-legged, at the other end of Smith Field, and I smelled fresh coffee. "You see what I've done," she said. "I've installed a percolator here at the corner. We weren't using this corner at all."

"You're a genius," I admitted.

"I've got another idea," she said. "When the new television sets come out, we can put a screen down here at the bottom of the field, and on Saturday afternoons we can lie in bed and watch the football games."

"Some day," I warned, "people will find out about the way we live, and will put us on exhibition."

The phone rang, and Marge picked up the extension. "It's Maria Ostenheimer," she said, puzzled, "for you."

I took the telephone, and said, "Hello, Maria, what are you doing for a living nowadays?"

"That's not very funny," the lady obstetrician said. "I've got a good mind not to tell you what I called about."

There was excitement in her voice. I said: "Go ahead, Maria, talk."

"Stephen," she said, "listen carefully. A baby is going to be born—may have been born already—in Tarrytown."

"Now Maria," I said, "just last week I flew down to a place called Big Stone Gap, Virginia, on one of those tips, and we landed in a cornfield and ground-looped, and it turned out to be a baby, all right, but a baby born to a circus elephant named Priscilla."

"Stephen," said Maria, enunciating her words slowly and carefully, "this is the real thing. You will remember I mentioned Dr. Blandy, who practises in Westchester. He was called on this case four months ago, back in May."

"Why didn't he mention it before?" I demanded.

"You dunce!" Maria said. "At first he thought it was going to be an abnormally small baby, and after the end of June he thought it might be an unusually long pregnancy. He didn't want to say a word about it until he was absolutely sure."

"And is he sure now?"

"There can be no doubt of it. The baby was conceived exactly nine months ago—three months after those damn uranium rays sterilized all the men. Blandy brought all the records of the case to my office this morning."

"Why did he bring them to you?" I asked, looking for a loophole I was sure existed.

"I am," said Maria, "on the executive board of the New York City investigating committee for the N.R.P. Besides, he knew there would be a great deal of publicity after the baby was born, and he wanted my advice. I said," she continued sarcastically, "that I might persuade you to handle the press, since you had some experience along those lines, and were sometimes considered reliable."

"Bless you! Maria. Bless you!" I exclaimed.

"What's going on here?" Marge interrupted.

"Quiet!" I shouted.

"You're not going to leave me out of this," Marge said. She went to the closet and took out a blue dress. Then she began to pull underthings out of a drawer.

"Maria," I said into the phone, "where is this child being born?"

There was a pause, and I knew she was searching for a memorandum. I considered all the things that J.C. would want me to do. "The address," Maria said, "is The Gatehouse, Rosemere, Tarrytown."

"That sounds like an estate," I said.

"It sounds like the gatehouse on an estate," Maria amended. "You'd better get going, Stephen, because it may happen any time this afternoon, according to Blandy. And remember, I'm depending on you to help him out."

My pajamas were off before I was out of bed. "I never," said Marge, startled, "saw you move so fast in all my life before."

"Throw some shirts and socks and shorts and my shaving kit and handkerchiefs into a bag," I yelled. "A baby is being born!"

"Where are we going?" she asked.

"Tarrytown."

"But that's only—"

"If this thing is true, I'm going to stay."

"You mean *we* are going to stay. This is just as important for me as it is for you. More!" I could see that Marge was already dressed, and was packing two bags, swiftly and efficiently, as if we were off for the weekend, and the train was going to leave in twenty minutes.

We caught a cab on Fifth Avenue, and the lights were with us all the way to Grand Central. The next train for Tarrytown was the Croton local. I bought a paper, and we fidgeted over a couple of milk shakes until it left.

It was an absurd train that crawled up the Hudson, pausing like a crosstown trolley at every intersection. I ticked off the stations— Glenwood, Greystone, Hastings-on-Hudson, Dobbs Ferry. Finally there came Irvington, and the next stop was Tarrytown.

There was a taxi at the station. "Do you know," I asked the driver, "where Rosemere is? I think it's an estate."

The hackman removed the stub of a cigar from his mouth. "Sure," he said, "been living here all my life. You want to go to Rosemere?"

"That's right," I said, throwing the bags into the back seat.

"Don't you want to put them in the trunk compartment?" the driver asked.

"No!" I said. "No! They are perfectly okay."

"You're in an awfully big hurry, fellow," the driver ventured.

I didn't say anything. I kept wondering what sort of people lived in the gatehouse. Probably, I thought, servants. Probably a butler and an upstairs maid had had some sort of an affair.

"Stephen," Marge said, "sit back and take it easy. You can't make it go any faster."

We crawled up the hill, and the cab stopped before stone gate-posts with a chain stretched between them, and a gravel drive beyond. "You want to go to the big house?" the hackman asked. "I hear it's closed up. The people go South this time every year."

"No," I said. "The gatehouse."

He unhooked the chain, and the cab crept up the driveway for fifty yards. The gatehouse was a compact, squat, two-story cottage, solidly constructed of field stone, with a mangy oak arched over the faded red tiles of its roof. There was a forty-six Buick sedan parked in front, with the little green marker that identifies the physician attached to its license plate. I gave the hackman a dollar, he backed down the driveway, and I pushed the bell and then knocked loudly on the door.

The door swung open, and Marge and I entered, carrying our weekend bags. "You're Smith," said a stocky, red-faced, perspiring man, perhaps forty-five, perhaps fifty. He was coatless, and his sleeves were rolled to his elbows. He looked as if he had been working.

"I'm Smith," I said, "and this is Mrs. Smith."

"How d'you do," he said, "I'm Blandy. Can't shake hands. Just washed 'em. Ostenheimer told me about you. She didn't say anything about Mrs. Smith."

"I just horned in," said Marge. "If I'm in the way—"

"Not at all. I've got a good nurse upstairs, but there are plenty of things you can do later. Anyway, your first job is to take care of him." Blandy nodded towards a corner which I had dismissed as being inhabited completely by a grand piano. Then he puffed up the steps.

In the corner, half-hidden by the piano, and seated on a green hassock, utterly uncomfortable and miserable, with his long chin cupped in his hands, and his knees and elbows askew, was a man. I said, "Hello."

"Hello," he said, and got to his feet, unbelievably stretching out to some six feet plus four or five or even six inches. "I'm Adam."

"You're what?"

"Adam. Homer Adam."

"You're the—"

"Yes, I'm going to have a baby. I mean Mary Ellen is." He kept putting his hands into his coat pockets and taking them out again. They were long, bony hands, and they were trembling. His shock of bright red hair appeared to be attempting to fly off his scalp in all directions.

"Now, look, fellow," I said with what I believed to be cheerful confidence, "take it easy. My name is Steve Smith, from the AP. I'm here to help you. Don't be so nervous. You'd think there'd never been a baby born before."

"There hasn't been, recently," Adam said. "That's just it."

Marge, who had been prowling the room, examining the hunting prints, the fireplace, the bookcases, and the curtains, giggled. "I like him," she said to nobody in particular. "He's nice."

From the upstairs came a sharp, feminine cry, suddenly bitten off in the middle. Adam began to shake. He collapsed on the sofa, and I was startled by the small number of cubic feet he occupied, sitting down, contrasted with his height, standing up.

"Look, Homer," I said, sitting down beside him, "I'm going to have to ask you a lot of questions, so I might as well start now."

Marge produced highballs, and an hour later she appeared with sandwiches. Just after dark the sounds from upstairs became more businesslike, and then Dr. Blandy shouted: "Hey, down there. It's all over. It's a girl—a fine girl! No trouble at all!"

"How much," I yelled back, "does she weigh?"

"What an inane question!" Marge said.

"I know, but you always ask it first."

Dr. Blandy shouted: "She's average and normal. When they're average and normal I always say they weigh seven pounds."

I walked to the phone on the hall table and called Circle 6-4111, and asked for Pogey. "J.C.," I said, "here is a flash." I enunciated each word clearly: "Flash—a girl baby was born to Mr. and Mrs. Homer Adam in Tarrytown, New York, at"—I glanced at my watch—"six fifty-one today!"

"You sane and sober, Steve?" J.C. inquired.

"Certainly."

"Did you say Adam?"

"Honest to Christ, J.C., it is Adam A-D-A-M."

"You will," J.C. ordered quietly, "give me a bulletin to follow flash within five minutes. You will then dictate a complete story, and don't hesitate to call in with new leads and inserts. Why this is the biggest story—"

"Since the Creation," I suggested.

"No," he said quietly, "just the biggest since Mississippi."

CHAPTER 3

The history of Homer Adam, until the day he became the world's lone post-Mississippi father, would not have earned him more than a three-paragraph obituary in his home-town newspaper, even if he had died an unusual and violent death.

He was born in Hyannis, Nebraska, a small but prosperous cattle town. His great-grandfather had crossed the plains in a covered wagon (something of which the editorial writers made much when the repopulation schemes were being considered). His grandfather was a cattleman, and his father was a wholesale grocer.

As a boy he was rather shy, and spent more time collecting stamps and Indian artifacts than he did playing football or riding and hunting. "You see," he confided in me, "I was much too tall for my age. The older, but smaller boys used to beat me up. I think it gave me an inferiority complex."

He wanted to be an archeologist, but his parents didn't think it was practical. He compromised on geology, and they sent him to the Colorado School of Mines, where his record was good enough to get him a job with the Guggenheims immediately after graduation. When war came, the Draft Board doctors, examining his gangling form, at first classified him as 4-F, but he probably would have attained 1-A eventually had not the government found a use for his special qualifications and dispatched him to Australia.

Living in a little mining town planted in the desert near Alice Springs made him homesick, and he became a prodigious letter writer. He wrote all his letters to Mary Ellen Kopp, a secretary in the Guggenheims' New York office. When he returned from Australia they were married, after a suitable engagement period.

These were the main facts, as he gave them to me while we sat in the living room of the gatehouse, waiting for his baby to arrive. However, they were not the principal things I wanted to know, but the birth of the Adam daughter interrupted my questioning.

It was not until much later—after Mr. Adam had seen his baby, and Marge had gone back to our West Tenth Street apartment (because there would be no room for her in the gatehouse that night) and I had peeped in on the mother and baby—that I found an opportunity to ask Homer the really pertinent questions.

We were sitting in the living room, and I had shoved another highball into Homer's hand, and had complimented him on both his wife and his child. Mary Ellen was a buxom, lusty young woman who, Dr. Blandy assured me, had gone through childbirth with considerable fortitude. "It was simple," he said, "as popping a peanut out of the shell." And the baby, as newborn babies go, could be classified as cute.

"I'm sorry," I explained, "that I have to ask all these questions at this time. I know—and it's quite natural too—that you're excited and upset. But it will save you a lot of trouble in the end, because you'll only have to answer them one time. All the reporters in New York will descend on this place before long, and I don't know who else besides, and if you give me all the answers I can handle them. This way, it won't bother you or your wife."

Homer shuddered, like a tall, thin, unkempt pine in a fitful breeze, and swallowed his drink. "Why did this have to happen to me?" he moaned.

"Don't be a damn fool," I said. "You're a very lucky and remarkable man. Why, you're the luckiest guy on earth."

"But what I cannot figure out," Homer said, "is how it happened. Please give me another drink. I think I ought to get tight, because you see I'm scared."

I poured him another drink, more rye than soda. He took a swallow and choked on it, water filling his eyes. "Easy!" I cautioned. "Just tell me, where were you on the day Mississippi exploded?"

"In Colorado," Homer replied. "The boss sent me to investigate the possibility of reopening some old silver and lead workings."

"Exactly where in Colorado?"

"Well, near Leadville. I spent the whole day in the lowest level of Eldorado No. 2. You know that's one of the deepest shafts in the world. Certainly the deepest lead workings. I was very much surprised when I went into Leadville that night—it was a Sunday—and they told me about the flash in the sky, and later I heard on the radio about the explosion."

I didn't have to know as much about physics as Professor Pell to guess the reason for Homer Adam's miracle. "When the explosion came," I said, "you were probably completely shielded from the world by lead?"

Mr. Adam considered this. "Yes," he said finally, "I suppose I was. The lead and silver ore in the lowest level is as rich as you'll find anywhere in the world. Hardly economical, though, because of—"

"Let's forget about it, from the mining viewpoint," I suggested. "Let's consider it from the viewpoint of the rays from the explosion."

"If lead protects you against radioactive rays," said Homer, "I suppose I was better protected, more than a mile down there, than any other man in the world."

"It certainly seems so," I said, "considering the known facts. Was there," I asked hopefully, wondering whether any other still potent males existed, "anybody else down there with you?"

"Oh, no," Homer replied. "You see Eldorado No. 2 has been abandoned for a generation or more. There are watchmen at the mine, but they only operate the elevators, and guard the machinery, and inspect the shafts for drainage. They rarely go into the lower levels."

The next few days, I would just as soon forget. It was like the Dionne quintuplets all over again, except that in this case it was the father, not the mother, in the center ring. There were other considerable differences, and one of them was that every human being, without exception, had a vital interest in Mr. Adam. I describe it inadequately. For the human race, the welfare and future of Mr. Adam was literally a matter of life and death.

I was hounded, harassed, heckled, harried, quizzed, questioned, cross-examined, badgered, and browbeaten by the ladies and gentlemen of my own profession until I did not know which end was up, or care much.

The first thing I did was borrow a technique that had proved successful in war coverage. I instituted a photographic pool system. This simply meant that instead of dozens of photographers swarming over the gatehouse, one still photographer and one newsreel cameraman were chosen by lot. They made pictures for all companies, newspapers, and agencies.

I arranged press conferences for Homer Adam, Mary Ellen, Dr. Blandy, and Mrs. Brundidge, the tight-lipped trained nurse who took a Scottish general attitude of disapproval regarding all these proceedings. Mrs. Brundidge was even persuaded to exhibit the baby (named Eleanor, for the mother was a firm Democrat). At the same time I managed to furnish the AP with enough exclusive material to keep J.C. Pogey satisfied, and yet not so much that other newspapermen would raise a beef that would exclude me from my strategic post in the gatehouse. Altogether, as I was to learn, I made a pretty satisfactory public relations counsel.

The press conferences, as can be imagined, were largely biological, but how else can a story like this be handled?

Shy as he was, and awkward, standing first on one leg and then on the other like a peculiar species of redheaded crane, Homer sometimes exhibited unexpected spunk and wit. Like when a sly, cynical, harridan from one of the tabloids asked him: "Now, Mr. Adam, not that it's wrong, but did you and your wife by any chance have premarital relations?"

Homer took a breath and replied, without anger: "You use awfully big words, ma'am. If you mean did we sleep together before we were married, the answer is no."

She jumped, and the other reporters laughed, and this annoyed her, and she said: "I was only endeavoring to discover whether this child might not have been the result of an exceptionally long pregnancy."

"That would have been sort of difficult," said Homer, "because almost up to the very day we were married Mary Ellen was in New York, and I was in Colorado."

"Well," said this unwholesome adjective artist, "there is also such a thing as extra-marital relationships!"

I had the answer to that one, but I wanted to see the creature hang herself, so for the moment I remained quiet. Homer stood very still, his long, bony hands white and twisting, and no color in his face. Then Mike Burgin, from the *Times*, said: "Look, madame"— and the way he pronounced "madame" left no doubt as to what sort of madame he meant—"I think you are out of line, and anyway this kid has already got red hair just like her father."

"My desk," the dough-faced witch alibied, "told me to ask."

"Well, just so your desk will not work itself into a lather," I interrupted, "tell your desk that we have already run complete blood tests, and Homer Adam is undoubtedly the pappy."

After the press was reasonably satisfied, the Army moved in. The American Army, when it has a war to fight, is an aggressive, eager, brainy, and enormously efficient organization. But when there is no war, the Army is something less than that. I suspect that its higher echelons are staffed, except for the professional soldiers, by gentlemen fearful of facing the competition of civilian life, officers to whom the barracks has become a nice, safe refuge.

The Army moved in first, with a platoon of Military Police dispatched from Fort Totten, after the Tarrytown Police Department, overworked and bewildered, sent out urgent distress signals. The MP's found a job to do, and they did it. They kept traffic moving outside the estate, and they shooed away the over-inquisitive who climbed fences, and sometimes frightened Mrs. Brundidge by staring through the kitchen windows, bug-eyed, while she mixed Eleanor's formula.

Perhaps their most arduous and interesting chore was acting as buffers, between Homer Adam and the teen-age girls who had, en masse, deserted a crooner known as "The Larynx," and a screen actor called "The Leer." Why it was no man can explain, but the photographs of Homer Adam definitely registered sex appeal to excitable, half-matured, single females. Until the MP's established a *cordon sanitaire* around the estate, their uninhibited tactics frightened Homer into the shakes, alarmed Mary Ellen, and disturbed the baby's digestion. They shocked Homer into the shattering knowledge that he was no longer—and probably never would be again—a private citizen enjoying the Fifth Freedom—Privacy.

But with the arrival of Colonel Merle Phelps-Smythe at Rosemere, Homer began to understand fully his future role in the national, and possibly the world scene.

Homer and I were playing gin and Blandy was kibitzing when the colonel put his riding boots and spurs through the door. "Who's in charge here?" he boomed. "I'm here to see Mr. Adam!"

"Why nobody's in charge," Homer said, rising derrick-like, "but I'm Adam."

"Well, now, that's why I'm here," Phelps-Smythe explained. "I'm here just exactly for that reason—because nobody's in charge. That's why the Army sent me to take over." He stated his name with some formality, and added: "I am the personal aide and Public Relations Officer of the Commanding General, Eastern Defense Command, Zone of the Interior. From now on"—he poked a fat forefinger at Homer's throat—"you are under the protection of the Eastern Defense Command. General Kipp is personally responsible for your safety, and I am personally responsible to General Kipp."

He glared at Blandy and me as if he had just, single-handed and above and beyond the call of duty, saved Homer Adam from violence at our hands. I glared back. There is nothing a Smith abhors so thoroughly as a hyphenated Smythe.

I would not have liked this hyphenated Smythe in any case. He had, somehow, without the aid of a single combat decoration, made his chest resemble a triple rainbow. He wore the Victory Ribbon from that old war, the pre-Pearl Harbor ribbon, and the American, European, and Asiatic Theater ribbons. But since no battle stars bloomed on these ribbons, they appeared to me like the gaudy hotel stickers that the tourists of the thirties exhibited on their luggage after doing Europe in three weeks. In addition, he wore various exotic decorations that I vaguely associated with Uruguay, the Dominican Republic, and the World's Fair. Under these, dangled ladders of shooting badges, indicating that he was a second-class pistol shot from the back of a horse, and a fair to middling rifle shot, prone. There was an unidentified sunburst on the right side of his stomach, just where the fat would be oozing out from under the ribs, had it not been for his obvious girdle.

"How," I inquired, "does the Eastern Defense Command go about taking over Mr. Adam?"

"In the first place—" the Colonel began, and then said: "You're that AP man who has been messing up the publicity. Who authorized you to be here anyway?"

"Me," said Homer meekly. "I did."

Blandy laughed. "And isn't this Mr. Adam's house?" he asked.

For a moment Phelps-Smythe was repulsed by this unexpected show of resistance, but he quickly recovered.

"In the first place," he said, "perhaps you do not know it, but the Joint Chiefs of Staff have decided, in the national interest, that Mr. Adam is vital, strategic government property. The Joint Chiefs felt themselves authorized in making this decision on the basis of future national defense."

"Congress," logically concluded Dr. Blandy, "has been demanding that the Administration do something about poor Homer, here, and that was the only thing they could think up to do."

Homer sat down, his mild blue eyes blinking. "But I don't wish to be taken over," he protested. "I just want to be left alone with Mary Ellen and the baby. Is it my fault that all the rest of you are sterile?"

Phelps-Smythe put his hand on Homer's drooping shoulder. "Now, my boy," he said, "remember this is in the national interest. Consider—you are just as much a military secret as the atomic bomb."

"Please don't mention atomic bombs," I said, remembering what Mississippi had done to our future, "I'm allergic to them."

"Besides," the colonel went on, ignoring me, "your wife and child will be taken care of until the present emergency is over. Funds have already been provided."

"I'm not going to leave Mary Ellen and the baby!" said Homer with some determination. "That, I simply won't do!"

"You won't have to leave immediately. You don't have to go to Washington until the hearings."

"What hearings?"

"The Congressional hearings on what to do with you. You see, the Joint Chiefs have simply declared you are vital and strategic. The War Department was entrusted with your safety, and my commanding general was given the job. But your final disposition will not be decided until after the Congressional hearings."

Homer looked dazed and helpless. "I see," he murmured.

"You're pretty lucky at that," said the colonel. "At first, we were going to put you down with the gold in Fort Knox. But the Surgeon General decided it might be bad for your health. Now that I've seen you in person, I think he was probably right. You weren't in the Army, were you?"

"No," said Homer. "I wasn't in the Army. The FEA sent me to Australia to locate quartz crystals. They were needed for radar."

"Well," said the colonel, "it's too bad you weren't in the Army, but I guess that radar tieup will show you're okay. I mean you weren't a conscientious objector, anyway."

"No, I wasn't a conscientious objector. Please, can I go upstairs and see Mary Ellen?"

"Well, make it snappy," the colonel ordered. "I've got a lot of papers for you to fill out. Incidentally, I'm taking you out to dinner tonight. My commanding general wants to meet you."

I caught the next train back to the city. I found J.C. in his office and told him that the Army had taken over, and my extra-curricular activities in Tarrytown had come to an end. I also told him I felt pretty sorry for Homer Adam.

"You'll feel sorrier," observed J.C., "when you see what happens to him in Washington!"

"How's that?" I asked.

"You've been too close to things in Tarrytown," J.C. surmised, "to keep up on what's been happening. First of all, there's a tug-of-war going on between the National Research Council and the National Re-fertilization Project as to who will get Adam."

"What do you mean, get him?"

"Well, both outfits think they can use Adam to start our birth rate going again. They've hinted at all sorts of schemes. Some of them don't sound completely unreasonable. At least they're no more unreasonable than what has already happened to us."

"Poor Adam!"

"That isn't all. There's a battle going on between Congress and an Inter-Departmental Committee as to who will decide policy on Adam. And that isn't all, either, because there is a quite powerful group which feels that the question of Adam is international, rather than national, and should be turned over to the United Nations."

"Quite a story, wasn't it," I mentioned, hinting at a bonus.

J.C. got that faraway look in his eyes, staring out over the masonry filled with pride that rises from the rock of Manhattan. "Quite a little fuss," he said. "We are indeed blind and naive if we believe that in this universe we will find living, feeling, happy, hurting, thinking creatures on this tiny sphere alone—this speck of an earth revolving around a dim star we call the sun, which is not even part of a constellation.

"It is as if an ant heap had been stamped down, and all the ants within cried that the world had come to an end."

Sometimes J.C. gave me the shivers.

CHAPTER 4

On a day in early December when an ice storm swept out of the northeast, and stiffened and slowed the arteries of Manhattan, and I knew that J.C. Pogey would want staffers covering the damage on the Jersey coast, I developed a convenient chill and retired to Smith Field to wait out the weather.

There is no vacation so exciting, so satisfactory, relaxing, and inwardly pleasing as that of a small boy playing hookey from school. I made the most of it. I clad myself in the soft, blue, silken pajamas inherited from Lynn Heinzerling when we were roommates at the Hotel de la Ville, in Rome, and he was ordered to Czecho-Slovakia; the wonderful brocaded Arabian robe that Noel Monks had purchased on the Street Called Straight, in Damascus, and willed to me when he flew Indiaward; and the pliant red leather slippers, with upturned toes, that had cost me three dollars, American gold seal, in the medina in Casablanca.

I cast myself upon Smith Field, set coffee dripping, and opened a package of cigarettes and a bottle of rye. I touched a switch at the side of the bed, and on the television screen there appeared an oval blur, and then the blur resolved itself into the face of a man—a full-jowled, hearty man who looked as if all he did was attend World Series, Bowl games, the tennis championships at Forest Hills, and the international shooting matches at Camp Perry. It turned out that this was expert deduction, because the man said:

"This is Malcolm Parkinson. I am speaking to you from sun-drenched Hialeah Park, Miami, Florida, and in a few moments I am going to focus your television camera on this magnificent race course, and you will see—yes, see—the first event on today's program . . ."

I picked up the telephone and called Sam's Cigar Store, at Sixth Avenue and Tenth. "Send me," I requested, "a *Racing Form* and *Bob's Best Bets*."

"In this weather?" Sam demanded.

"The horses," I pointed out, "are not running up the Avenue of the Americas."

"That I know," said Sam. "That I can see from here." He asked: "Tell me, Mr. Smith, why don't they do something about Mr. Adam?"

"Who do you mean by they?"

"Them bureaucrats."

"What," I inquired, "would you have them do?"

"The missus keeps pestering me," said Sam. "She believes in A.I." A.I. had become the popular abbreviation for artificial insemination.

"Well, there's bound to be a decision soon," I assured him.

"There better be, or there'll be hell to pay in this country. My wife says she's not getting any younger. I tell you, Mr. Smith, she wants kids."

When the *Racing Form* arrived I began to dope the horses at Hialeah. Like every frustrated sports writer, I believe I am a better handicapper than any now operating at the tracks. I picked Fair Vision in the second, and then called "Two Tone Jones," a gentleman of doubtful color who operates a bookmaking establishment near Sheridan Square. I bet two across the board on Fair Vision, poured myself a rye, and settled back on the pillows to watch the race.

I found that watching the races, from a bed in New York, was more satisfactory than watching them at the track, in Florida. Maniacs do not jump up and down in front of you, deafening you with their shrill cries, and interfering with your vision. Nobody picks your pocket. Nobody tramps on your feet. You don't have to butt your way to the parimutuel windows, tramping on other people, between each race. You don't have to foam at the mouth while crawling through traffic jams, park your car, pay $2.20 admission, avoid touts, buy programs, pencils, and peanuts, or steer your wife away from the hundred-to-one shots. You don't have to shiver in a white linen suit, and try to warm yourself by talking about the cold wave up north.

You just lie there in bed and lose your money.

When I telephoned to place my bet on the fifth, Two Tone Jones said: "You got a minute, Mr. Smith? I want to ask you a question."

"Certainly," I said graciously, for by then Two Tone Jones was one of my considerable creditors.

"We're having a little argument up here," said Two Tone Jones. "You're a pretty smart man, Mr. Smith, and maybe you can help us out."

"I'm not very smart about picking horses."

"Oh," said Two Tone, "we all have our bad days. Now what we want to know, Mr. Smith, is what about this here artificial insemination?"

I drank some black coffee. "Well, what can I tell you about it?" I said. I was pretty sick of this A.I. It reminded me of toddle tops, ouija boards, every day in every way I feel better and better, two cars in every garage, life begins at forty, and every other fad that ever existed.

"Well, we just want to know about it," Two Tone complained.

"It is very simple," I said. "When normal intercourse isn't practical, you just take a specimen of the male sperm, and plant it within the female."

"Hasn't it been done with horses?" Two Tone asked.

"Oh, yes. Nowadays, when a horse is standing at stud, he doesn't have to service a mare in person. His sperm is shipped, injected, and that is all there is to it. Why, some of our best thoroughbred stock has been planted in Argentine and Australia that way. It's much easier to ship an ounce of sperm than a one-ton horse."

"Can it be done with men?" Two Tone demanded.

"Of course. I think there are eight thousand cases of artificial insemination recorded in this country."

"That's what we wanted to know."

"Don't you read the papers?" I asked. "The papers have been talking about nothing but A.I. ever since it was recommended by N.R.P."

"Well, we don't read that part of the papers," said Two Tone Jones. That was that. I bet twenty to win on Eastbound, in the fifth, and he finished absolutely last.

Marge returned home during the running of the sixth. Cliffdweller, which I had backed to win and place, was on the rail and leading by two lengths when Marge swung open the door of our bedroom. I hushed her with a wave of my hand. "And now as they come into the stretch," Malcolm Parkinson was saying, "it is still Cliffdweller, and he's running easy. He's followed by Ragtime, June Bug, Third Fleet, and Firefly . . . now at an eighth from the wire Cliffdweller still leads but—"

"Stephen Decatur Smith," Marge interrupted, "we have company!"

"Quiet!" I shouted, leaning forward, pounding my knees with my fists as Cliffdweller labored towards the finish. At this point, it seemed that the television screen had shifted to slow motion.

"Stephen!" Marge shouted.

The horses crossed the finish line. "It's a photo!" shouted Parkinson. I fell back against the pillow.

"So this is why I haven't been able to get you on the telephone all afternoon!" Marge said. "Sneaked off to the races!"

I looked up at her. She was remarkably businesslike and trim and tidy in a blue suit and a white blouse that concealed, and yet promised, the smooth curves underneath. She was a very admirable-looking woman, but she was very angry. In a case like this, I believe that the best defense is an offense. "Here I am, down in bed with a chill, and I get abused!" I reproached her.

Marge smiled, and touched my forehead lightly with her fingers. She knew that I wasn't ill, and she knew that I knew that she knew. "Come on! Get off the Field and into the living room. I brought home some people."

Parkinson's cheerful, weathered face appeared on the screen. "Who?" I asked absent-mindedly.

"In just a second," said Parkinson, "the judges will have inspected the picture, and we will have the result of the sixth. Meanwhile, let me tell you that I've never seen Hialeah more colorful than it is today, here in the bright sunshine, with the brilliant plumage of the famous flamingoes out by the lake. And remember that for relaxation like a trip to the Southland, always smoke—"

"That man is a bad influence on you," Marge interrupted. "Shoo him away. Anyway, it gives me the creeps to have strange men in the bedroom, staring at us."

"Here's the results," said Parkinson. "It's Cliffdweller, by a whisker."

I flicked the switch and rolled off Smith Field, feeling better. Out in the living room, their faces flushed by the cold wind, Maria Ostenheimer and my friend of the Apennines and Polyclinic, Dr. Thompson, were standing close to the fire. "Hello," I greeted them, "didn't know you two knew each other."

"Our acquaintanceship," said Thompson, "is strictly professional—at least thus far." Maria, delicately made, looked almost childlike alongside his bulk. "We're on the same committee," she explained.

Marge inspected me thoughtfully, tapping a cigarette on the mantel. "They've just come from Washington," she said. "They appeared before both the Executive Inter-Departmental group and the Joint Congressional Committee on behalf of the National Refertilization Project. They testified for A.I."

"Well, Maria did," amended Thompson. "I'm more interested in another aspect of the problem."

"All I've heard today," I complained, "is A.I." A startling, and horrible possibility gripped me. I pointed my finger at Marge. "If you think for one instant," I told her, "that we are going to fill this apartment with lanky, redheaded children all subject to inferiority complexes, and none of them mine, then you had better start thinking again. You're not going to be any female guinea pig to test the productive capacity of Mr. Adam!"

Thompson threw back his head and laughed. "Relax, Steve," he said. "Relax!"

"Anyway," said Marge, acidly, "I understand that Washington has been simply snowed under with applications. There are thousands ahead of me, even if I wanted an Adam child. There are plenty of husbands whose sense of responsibility to the human race is greater than their selfishness and stupid jealousy!"

Maria cocked her head on the side and looked at me with her wise, dark eyes. "I have just finished telling our distinguished statesmen," she said, "that A.I. may be the only salvation for mankind. I say may"—her words tripped out slowly and daintily, as if they were being carefully marched across a narrow plank—"I say may because right at present A.I. is the only solution which we *know* will work. Artificial insemination is bound to furnish at least a limited number of males in another generation."

"Can you imagine," I exclaimed, "the whole world peopled with redheaded beanpoles, all looking exactly like Homer Adam!"

"But that's not why we came to see you," Maria said, and for a small, quite pretty and young girl she was alarmingly grave. "We came to see you about Homer Adam himself."

"What's the matter?" I asked. "Is he pining away without his Mary Ellen?"

"Well, something like that," Maria said, still grave and troubled. "You see, this business has naturally been a very great shock to him. And they mauled and manhandled him fearfully when he got to Washington."

"That Phelps-Smythe!" said Thompson. "The first thing the Eastern Defense Command did to Adam was fill him up with shots until he was a walking pharmaceutical encyclopedia. They shot him full of paratyphoid, typhus, yellow fever, influenza, cholera—as if he were going to catch cholera at Fort Myer—smallpox, and I don't know what else besides."

"Phelps-Smythe," I remarked, "is a revolving son-of-a-bitch."

"And all the brass exhibits poor Mr. Adam at dinners," said Maria, "as if he were a freak."

"Phelps-Smythe," I said, "is bucking for a star. If he pleases enough generals, maybe one day he'll get to be a general himself. Ask any correspondent who was in the Southwest Pacific. They'll tell you how it works. They had a beaut out there."

Thompson held out his huge hands, six inches apart. "Adam," he said, "is now no wider than that. Furthermore, he has developed a twitch."

"It is really very serious," said Maria. "As things are now, everything depends on the well-being of one man—a sensitive man who apparently was never very strong. If his health is ruined—either his physical health or his mental health—it imperils the chances of successful artificial insemination.

"Let me put it this way. Our present methods of A.I. are still fairly crude. It is true that you will find millions of motile sperm cells in one male specimen, but we have not yet found a way to isolate these cells—keep each one of them alive, happy, and potent so that each one has a chance of causing pregnancy. Artificial insemination is still a matter of mass impregnation. You use millions of cells, but only one does the job."

"What a waste!" I said.

"What a waste indeed, at this period in history," said Marge.

"Well, we're working on the isolation problems, but meanwhile we want to start A.I. as quickly as possible," Maria continued. "Suppose something happened to Homer Adam before we began? Anyway, we can not make maximum—perhaps not even normal—use of Homer Adam until he again becomes a tranquil, normal man. Even if we were able to use him in his present state—which is doubtful—we might create a race of physical and nervous wrecks."

I didn't sense what was coming. "What," I inquired, "has this got to do with me?"

"I talked to Adam," said Thompson. "He likes you, he trusts you, and he wonders what became of you. You made a very deep impression on him. What did you do?"

"Nothing," I replied, "except let him beat me at gin rummy occasionally."

Thompson grinned. "There is nothing so good for a man's ego as to believe himself a shark at gin," he said.

"In any case," Maria concluded, "if the government decides that N.R.P. be placed in charge of Homer Adam, rather than the N.R.C., we want you to handle him."

"Oh my God!" I said. "Nominated to be nursemaid to the potential father of his country!"

The controversy between the National Re-fertilization Project and the National Research Council was essentially between the physicians and the physicists—between the scientific workers in the animate and the inanimate fields. The atom-poppers believed they needed Mr. Adam for research which they hoped would undo the damage caused by the obscure rays which enwrapped the world after the Mississippi explosion. They needed Mr. Adam, they explained, much as they needed cyclotrons and centrifuges.

How could an antidote to the ray be developed until they knew exactly which ray had done the trick? And how could they isolate the ray which strangely wrecked male cells, and left females undisturbed, unless they had specimens for experimentation? And who was there, except Mr. Adam, to furnish these specimens?

The N.R.P. physicians pointed out, even as Maria had, that A.I. was the only sure way of keeping the globe populated. They hoped that the physicists of N.R.C. would find a method of restoring the potency of all men, but scientific research takes times. Meanwhile, they had on hand one single, priceless human who was insurance against entire extinction.

What finally decided the Joint Congressional Investigating Committee, and the Inter-Department Executive Committee, I am sure, was the unspoken fear that the scientists would make another mistake, mess up Mr. Adam, and then everybody would be finished. It was something that nobody spoke of, directly, for fear of injuring the sensibilities of men like Professor Pell, and damaging their professional reputation, but the fear was always there.

So I was not surprised, a few days later, when I picked up a copy of the New York *Post* while walking to the subway after my noon breakfast in Smith Field, to read the black headlines that covered the whole front page:

PRESIDENT OKAYS A.I.!
N.R.P. WINS OVER N.R.C. BUT SCIENTISTS TO GET
FUND TO CONTINUE RESEARCH
WOULD-BE MOTHERS VOLUNTEER THROUGHOUT
NATION
ENGLAND ASKS AID

When I reached the office, J.C. set me to putting together the foreign reactions in a single story. As usual there was no official comment from Moscow, but *Pravda* printed an oblique little box on its front page pointing out that is was possible for the United States to make amends for the world catastrophe caused by Mississippi, but that thus far the United States had not approached the Soviet Union directly.

The word "directly" was the important word. It was seized upon, that very day, in the Senate. Had anybody in the Administration, certain Senators wished to know, been dealing secretly on sharing Homer Adam with the Communists? If so, what arrangements had been discussed? It was hoped that Homer Adam would not be shipped outside the territorial limits of the United States.

Senator Salt plausibly replied that A.I. being what is was, it was not necessary to ship Homer Adam anywhere, just the male germ.

Any peace-loving nation, Salt said, could be helped out without Homer ever leaving Washington. Russia had as much right to hope for perpetuating herself as any other nation—more than some he could mention.

FROGHAM (D. Louisiana): Will the Senator yield?

SALT: I yield.

FROGHAM: Is it not a fact that we could forever dispose of this damnable Communism, which is infecting the whole world and causing strikes and disturbances and menacing the very foundations of the Republic, say within two generations, by simply confining A.I. to those nations which are willing to give us definite statements as to their future foreign policies, and their territorial and ideological intentions?

VIDMER (R. Massachusetts): If we only give A.I. to those nations which know their future foreign policy, then we will have to exclude the United States. (Laughter.)

The story from London was matter-of-fact. England expected

that the United States would share A.I., on a population basis, and in return England would give the United States the full benefit of any happy information reaching its own scientists. The British government felt it was speaking for the whole Empire. It didn't say anything about Ireland.

In Paris, all the newspapers published editorials pointing out France's great past cultural contributions to the world, and insisting that it was a necessity that French culture continue.

Various good Germans talked of the benefits of a revival of German industrial genius in succeeding generations.

The Japanese press talked of traditional American sportsmanship, and pointed out that baseball was played in both countries.

All the little nations extolled their own virtues. But the Bucharest press pointed out, coyly, that if A.I. was denied to Hungary, then that would be a final solution to the question of Transylvania—which everybody thought had already been solved.

The cables kept rolling in, but before night J.C. Pogey came over to my desk, and motioned me into his office.

"Steve," he said, "I just got a call from the White House. Danny Williams—the President's Secretary. Used to work for us. Well, they want you down there to handle Adam."

"That's what I was afraid of," I said.

"It seems they think you did a good job in Tarrytown. Adam likes you."

"Yeah?"

"The N.R.P. asked for you. They're going to put you on their payroll. We'll give you leave of absence."

"Haven't I got anything to say about this?" I demanded.

"Not much," said J.C. "Danny Williams put it this way—he said it was in the interests of civilization. I don't like to lose you, but it is exactly the same as if you were drafted."

"You don't care much, do you, J.C., whether civilization keeps on or not?"

J.C. rubbed his thumbs behind his ears. "Dunno," he said. "Haven't made up my mind yet."

I went home and packed. "They certainly called for you in a hurry," Marge said.

"Yes," I agreed, not wanting to leave her, and not wanting to leave Smith Field, and wondering how long it would be before Homer Adam could be cooled off and calmed to a point where he would become useful to civilization, and N.R.P. would let me go.

"You behave down there," Marge commanded. "That town is full of good-looking women, and they don't seem to have any inhibitions any more."

"I'll behave," I promised.

"You'd better. I'm liable to pop in on you any time—any time at all. And Stephen," she added, "do a good job, will you. It's awfully important to me."

I telephoned to Abel Pumphrey, the Director of the National Re-fertilization Project, that I was on the way down. Marge took me to the train and kissed me goodbye as if I were off to Shanghai. The last thing she said was, "You will do your best, won't you?"

Women are such queer people.

CHAPTER 5

I didn't have any illusions about my chore. I knew that at the very best it would be thankless, and probably a perpetual headache, and something which called for a psychiatrist rather than a newspaperman. But I felt a sort of moral responsibility for Mr. Adam. I had been the first to launch him into his career as the last productive male, and it seemed only right that I should help guide his footsteps towards whatever strange destiny awaited him. In addition, I was just plain curious.

I underestimated Washington. I didn't foresee any of the really frightening events that presently engulfed me. When I look back at it now, I was a toddling child who picks a river in flood as a nice place for wading, and instantly is seized by the current and swept downstream.

For instance, I thought the National Re-fertilization Project would be composed of a dozen or so people, with a committee of physicians like Maria Ostenheimer and Tommy Thompson acting as advisers. It wasn't like that at all. The N.R.P. was an enormous chunk of government, expanding day by day. The creation of any new government agency is, in many respects, like bringing in a new oil field. With the N.R.P., to which the President had allotted unlimited emergency funds, it was as if gold had been discovered in California all over again.

The day on which I arrived in Washington—December 18—is eaten into my memory by the acid of shock, just as the men who were there will always remember the date of Anzio, or Omaha Beach.

I hadn't expected anyone to meet me at the station, but when I went through the gates into the concourse a neat young man with a pointed, thin, suspicious nose—the type of nose I always associate with credit managers—stopped me. "You're Mr. Smith?" he said.

"Uh-huh."

He held out his hand. "I'm Klutz—Percy Klutz, Deputy Director on the administrative side." When he smiled his mouth looked like that of a fresh-caught skate. "The Chief sent me down to meet you."

"That was nice of him," I said. The Chief would be Abel Pumphrey. I wondered how he had recognized me, and asked. He said the AP Bureau had produced a description, and a photograph. He wondered whether I'd had lunch, and when I told him no, he suggested Harvey's. Outside the station was a sedan, with a government seal, and N.R.P., stenciled on its door.

We ordered clams and steaks and then Klutz said: "I suppose this is as good a time as any to fill you in on the big picture. We're really beginning to build an organization, now. Everybody thinks the Chief is the coming man in the Administration. Of course, it has been an uphill fight all the way. First the Interior Department tried to take over, and then the Public Health Service claimed it was their baby. Right now we're operating under the Executive Office of the President, so we don't have much budget trouble. The real test will come when we go to Congress for regular annual appropriations. I guess our big break was when we got Adam away from the National Research Council."

"How is Homer Adam?" I inquired. "I'd like to see him as soon as possible."

He looked at me, curiously, and then took a pencil from an inside pocket and began drawing a chart on the tablecloth. "Now up at the top, of course," he went on, ignoring my question, "is the President, and right under the President—" his deft pencil drew a little box and began filling it with names—"is the Inter-Departmental Advisory Committee. They decide top policy."

"On what?" I asked. "I thought the idea was simply to get Adam in shape, and then start producing babies."

"Oh, no!" Klutz said, startled. "The production end is only the smallest part of it! That comes way down here—" he indicated the bottom of the tablecloth—"in Operations."

"Now as you see," he went on, "the top policy group is composed of the President himself, the Secretaries of State, War, Interior, and Navy—I don't know why they put in Navy except that they put in War—the Surgeon General, Director of National Research Council—we couldn't keep him off it—and finally the Chief."

A strange light came into Klutz's eyes, and he began to sketch more boxes, connected by lines horizontally and vertically, with lightning precision. "Now right under the top policy group N.R.P. operates. I'm over here to the right of the Chief, and under me I've got Administration, Budget, Housing, Communications, and Transportation. I don't fool around with policy, planning, or operations. I'm just the man who keeps things running."

Klutz's pencil raced on. "Branching off this line that runs from the Chief up to top policy we have the liaison officers from the other departments or agencies—we're having a tough time finding suitable quarters for all of them—and directly under the Chief we have the Planning Board."

"Planning Board?"

"Certainly! You see, policy flows down to the Chief from the top group, and then down to the Planning Board, which is composed of our own heads of branches and divisions. The Planning Board issues the directives and passes them on down to be implemented. Right off the Planning Board, here, we have the Advisory Committee which is composed of leading physicians and biologists and such from all over the country. They aren't in government, of course. They're just to give us backing when we need it."

Klutz hadn't touched his clams, and he didn't seem to notice when the waiter whisked them off the table. "The Deputy Director falls right under the Planning Board, and out from him you have our own liaison officers, who operate on the Planning Level, including the one to Congress, and our own advisory group on international problems which communicates directly with the State Department and sends proposals to the Planning Board. You see how nicely the channels flow."

"Yes. I see." I found I was watching like a child fascinated by a sidewalk artist sketching the Battle of Bunker Hill.

"Right under the Deputy Director come the Assistant Directors for the various branches," Klutz went on. "Research and Analytical. Statistical. Public Relations. And of course, Operations. Then under the branches there come the various divisions, which I'll just sketch in here in small boxes, because I don't think they'd interest you just now."

"And where do I fit in?" I asked.

"Well, you see we've already got an Assistant Director for Public Relations—Gableman. Did you ever meet him?"

"No, I don't think so."

"He's a very fine newspaperman," Klutz said, in some surprise. "I think he started doing publicity for the WPA, and later he shifted to the National Youth Administration. I think he also wrote for NRA. Anyway, he was one of the young writers for the Office of Facts and Figures, and then he graduated to the OWI. He went to the State Department from the OWI, and we got him from them. Very fine newspaperman. Very experienced. He's building up an excellent branch. I'm giving them a building of their own very shortly."

"And me?"

"Well, frankly, you're rather a problem. You see we already have an Assistant Director for Public Relations, so we'll make you Special Assistant to the Director, and put you in here." He drew a line away from the line that connected Pumphrey to the Planning Board, and put a little box at the end of it, and wrote "Smith" inside the box. "I don't know whether you'll operate on the policy, or the planning, or the operations level," Klutz explained, "so in any case that will take care of it."

"Is Homer Adam in that little box with me?" I demanded.

Klutz appeared uneasy, as if the lunch he hadn't eaten wasn't agreeing with him. "Oh, no," he said, "Adam is way down here, at the bottom. You're way up at the top." In a little square at the end of Operations he wrote, "Adam."

I felt a powerful urge to finish my steak, leave the check for Klutz, and catch the next train back for New York, but instead I said, "Now look, bud. The only reason I came to this goddam town was to take care of Adam. If I'm not going to take care of Adam, say so now, and I'll be on my way. This wasn't my idea. It came from Adam first, and then from the White House."

When I mentioned the White House, Klutz gulped, and instantly his manner changed. "Oh, I'm sorry," he said. "I didn't know that."

I recognized Klutz as one of the public servants who has no equals. He has only superiors or inferiors. Everybody is neatly tagged either above him, or below him. He keeps his nose nestled close under the coattails of those above, and his feet firmly planted on the heads of those underneath, and if he maintains this balance for thirty years he gets a pension and retires to Chevy Chase. "Well, you know it now," I told him.

"I didn't bring up the matter of Adam," he explained, "because there seems to have been some confusion about him in the directives.

You see, when Adam was turned over to N.R.P. the Army still managed to keep a finger in the pie. They claimed that the presidential directive merely gave N.R.P. the use of Adam, but that his security was still a matter for the Army. We reached an agreement with the Army by which a committee was set up."

"Another committee!"

"Yes. It was set up simply to direct overall policy on Adam, personally, rather than Adam in the productive sense, and to hand down directives to the Operations Branch. I represented N.R.P. on the committee and Phelps-Smythe—"

"That bastard!" I remarked, and Klutz jumped.

"Well, he represented the Army. Phelps-Smythe and I reached an agreement that you could also sit on the committee."

I told him what I thought of such an arrangement in a few words, all short and Elizabethan, and Klutz said he thought Pumphrey should decide, and I told him we might as well have a showdown right away.

The National Re-fertilization Project was camped in a group of buildings near the intersection of 23rd and D streets, in Northwest Washington, and it spread out into temporary structures, lately abandoned by the Navy, that occupied adajacent parkland.

Within the Administration Building there was an impressive bustle—the scuttling back and forth of girl messengers, the clatter of a typist pool, the buzz of telephones, the passionate murmurs that rose from conference rooms. Through the building there was the smell of fresh paint, and a sense of growth and change.

A new government agency on the upgrade mushrooms within the capital like a tropical plant. Its growth is exotic and surprising as an orchid, but like a fungus it is a frail plant, likely to wither swiftly and die under the cold breath of Congress or the Bureau of the Budget.

But the offices of Abel Pumphrey were cut off from the surrounding uproar by soundproof walls, and furnished in the solid good taste of one who has been firmly fastened to the public teat for years. Abel Pumphrey's name kept appearing in the Congressional Directory long after the bureaus and agencies he headed became half-forgotten combinations of initials. He came to Washington as a liberal Republican, at the proper time switched to being a conservative Democrat, but he was born a bureaucrat. This means that he had thousands of acquaintances, no firm allegiances or convictions, no enemies, and probably no close friends with the possible exception of his wife.

He was picked as Director of N.R.P., immediately after W.S. Day, because he was considered "safe." There wasn't any other place to put him at the moment, and he had six children. At that time Mr. Adam had not been discovered, much less acquired by N.R.P., so the task of re-fertilization seemed more theoretical than practical. Now Pumphrey's post had suddenly become extremely important, and of the most consuming public interest, and Pumphrey was more than somewhat worried.

Outwardly, however, he seemed calm and cheery—an apple-red and apple-round man with a Herbert Hoover collar squeezing his neck—when he greeted me. "Well, well, Steve!" he said. We had never met before. "It's certainly fine of you to come down here and help us out. Fine! Fine! Percy here will get you all squared away. How about it, Percy?"

I didn't give Klutz a chance to speak. I said, "I'm afraid there's been some misunderstanding. I came here to get Adam on his feet. That's all. Nothing else. As far as I know, that's all the White House wants me to do."

Every time I said White House, Klutz jumped. I decided to say it more often. "Naturally," said Pumphrey. "I am in full accord with that. Didn't you explain, Percy?"

"I told him about the directive," Klutz said, "and the little committee we'd set up, and how he could sit on the committee."

I said, "No committees. I hate committees."

Pumphrey spread out his hands in a placating gesture. "Now

Steve," he said, "wouldn't it be better if there was a committee, even if you did all the work and made all the actual, ah—contacts? The protection of Adam is a very delicate matter, very delicate. Very delicate, and ticklish. If anything happened, if there was, ah—any scandal, wouldn't it be better if the War Department shared the responsibility?"

I said, "No."

Pumphrey drooped. "I suppose ultimately," he decided, "the responsibility is that of the President. After all, he picked you for this particular phase of our work. I'll ask him to clarify the directive. Or maybe I'd better not. I'm not sure that it's not clear now. Anyway, I'll call in Phelps-Smythe, and we'll tell him about it. Phelps-Smythe is the Army's liaison officer over here. He's been representing the Army on the committee, you know."

"I know," I said.

Phelps-Smythe hadn't changed since Tarrytown, neither he nor his ribbons. He knew what was up, of course, and by the way he talked I could tell he had discussed it with his general and decided upon a course of action. After Pumphrey explained that the committee was ended, he said, with the formality of a diplomat delivering a démarche to a hostile state:

"The War Department strongly disapproves of relaxing security measures for the protection of Homer Adam. The War Department wishes to point out that if anything happened to Adam the future of the nation would be endangered."

"What you mean," I interrupted, "is that there wouldn't be any future for the nation—or the world. Maybe that's why the President wants me, and not you, to handle Adam."

I shouldn't have said it, I guess, but I couldn't resist. Phelps-Smythe glared at me. I hoped he would have a stroke, but he didn't. Behind his desk Pumphrey began to nibble nervously at the edge of his lips.

"The War Department," Phelps-Smythe continued, "wishes a

written release of all responsibility for the safety and protection of Adam. The War Department wishes this release immediately, because we intend to withdraw our guards and security patrols from the Shoreham at 6 o'clock this evening."

"So that's where you've got Adam caged up?" I said.

Pumphrey didn't pay any attention. "Is the War Department going to make anything public on this?" he asked Phelps-Smythe.

"Naturally."

"But it's liable to start a lot of controversy."

"That is not the fault of the War Department!"

Pumphrey sagged like a toy balloon from which enough air has escaped so that it is no longer round and shining. "Very well," he sighed. "I'll send the release round to your office, Colonel, as soon as I get a chance to dictate and sign it."

"Thank you," said Phelps-Smythe, and left. I could have sworn he clicked his heels.

Immediately Klutz turned to Pumphrey. "I'd better find Nate," he said. "This looks like trouble."

It turned out that Nate was Gableman, the Assistant Director for Public Relations, a dark and cadaverous young man with his hair two inches longer than the barber ordinarily allows, and fingernails that matched his hair, both in length and color. His eyes ran over me in quick speculation and appraisal, he listened to Pumphrey's account of what had happened thus far, and he said, "I should have been cut in on this right away. What do you think a Public Relations man is for?"

"I'm sorry, Nate," Pumphrey said. "But it happened so fast."

"You haven't written that memorandum for Phelps-Smythe yet?"

"Oh, no. He just left."

Gableman's dark eyes came alive behind his spectacles. "Okay," he said. "We'll move in a hurry. I'll get out a special press release right away. You hold that memorandum until I'm ready. We'll get our story out first."

"What is our story, Nate?" Pumphrey asked.

"Why, it's very simple. Abel Pumphrey, Director of the National Re-fertilization Project, today announced that N.R.P. had taken over complete personal control of Mr. Adam from the War Department, at the President's request. You see, that puts the onus on the War Department. They can't buck the President. He's Commander in Chief. Then we say that Mr. Adam wasn't getting sufficient personal freedom under present conditions. He should have all the rights and freedoms of every other American. That gets us in good with the Liberals. Then we say that Steve Smith here has been appointed a Special Assistant to Mr. Pumphrey and entrusted with the safety of Adam. Smith and Adam are personal friends—you are, aren't you?"

"Hardly old friends," I said.

"Well, anyway, personal friends. That shows we have Adam's best interests at heart."

I could see that Gableman was a pretty smooth customer around the edges. He may have learned all his newspapering as a government press agent, but he was an expert in mimeograph warfare. "We might also hint," he went on, "just to get in a dig at the War Department, that Adam hasn't been doing so hot under the previous arrangement."

"Oh, I wouldn't do that!" Pumphrey protested. "It might bounce back on us as well as the War Department."

"I should say not," said Klutz.

"It could start rumors," said Pumphrey. "It could start a panic. Why you ought to see the letters I get from really big businessmen—I mean the very biggest—on the importance of Adam. Do you know what would happen if anything happened to Adam? Why the insurance companies would go bust. The effect on the market—inconceivable—"

"Okay," Gableman agreed. "I hadn't considered that angle. I'll get to work."

Klutz wanted me to take a look at my office, complete with

secretary, but I insisted on seeing Adam immediately. Pumphrey told me there would be plenty of room for me in Adam's suite. There would be plenty of room for a company of Marines, I gathered from the description.

This was correct. The Army hadn't yet withdrawn its security patrols when I arrived at the Shoreham. There was an armored car, and two weapon carriers mounting .50 calibre machine guns, strategically placed in the hotel's driveway. It turned out that Adam occupied the entire fifth floor of F wing. I had some trouble getting up there, because there were MP's posted in all the hallways and at the elevators, but the captain in charge had been informed I was on the way, and he finally agreed to let me go up a few minutes before six, when the Army's Operation Adam officially ended.

I found Adam in the living room customarily given over to the Duke of Windsor, visiting Indian rajahs, and presidents from the banana republics. For a hotel it is quite a room, gaudy with modern paintings, cream-colored furniture, and silky white rugs. Magazines and newspapers were tossed about it, however, so that at this moment it resembled the picnic grounds in Central Park at the end of a summer Sunday. On a folding serving table was an enormous tray loaded with lobster salad, shrimp, hors d'oeuvres, and pastries, all resting in untouched and pristine glory on heavy silver. A stuffed shirt of a voice, which sounded like Kaltenborn, boomed out of a wall radio like a muffled drum.

I saw a mop of red hair protruding over the back of an armchair. It was Adam. He was not asleep, nor could he be classified as being awake. He appeared to be in a half-comatose state, slumped in upon himself like a daddy longlegs at rest, his eyes glazed, and his mouth slack and open. Then he saw me, wobbled to his feet, and held out his hand. I admit I was shocked. He looked like one of those walking skeletons after seven years in Dachau. He said, "Steve! You finally got here. Jesus, I'm glad to see a human face!"

I tried to conceal my surprise at his wretched appearance. "Take it easy," I said. "From now on things are going to change. Let's have a drink."

"Oh, I'm not allowed to drink," said Homer. "Nothing but eggnogs. I get sick when I think of eggnogs. I'll never be able to look a hen in the face again."

"From now on," I told him, "you can have anything you damn well please—anything at all."

"Really?" he said. "Honest to God?" It was pretty pathetic. His hands were shaking, and tears had started into his eyes.

"You're damn right." I picked up a telephone, called room service, and ordered a case of rye. If ever a bundle of nerves needed alcoholic relaxation, it was Homer Adam.

He began to tell me the tale. "They treated me like a prize puppy dog. They wouldn't let me off this floor, except when they came to put me on exhibit. Then they'd dress me up, and lead me around to a party where I didn't know anybody, and show me off like I deserved the blue ribbon. I'm not a freak! I'm a normal human being."

"I'll say," I agreed.

"They'd discuss me like I was a stud horse—right in front of my face. How long I could be expected to produce, and whether they should inject testosterone, and stuff like that. It was embarrassing. You don't wonder I've been off my feed?"

"No, I don't wonder at all."

The rye arrived, and I poured Homer a big slug. He kept on talking, and I encouraged him. I'm no psychologist, but it was apparent there was a lot he had to get off his chest. It was part of the cure.

Finally he said, "I don't mind doing what I can. I suppose it's my duty. But they've got no right to keep me away from my family." His eyes misted again, like the eyes of a child who has been needlessly and wantonly injured. "I don't know if I ought to talk about it. It's sort of personal, Steve."

"You go ahead and talk, Homer," I said. "You tell me every little tiny thing. I'm here to listen."

"Well, it's me and Mary Ellen. She's the only girl I ever had. Know what I mean?"

I nodded. "Uh-huh." I didn't smile.

Homer poured himself a drink. I could see that what he had to say needed priming. I didn't try to hurry him. "When I say I never had a girl except Mary Ellen I mean it literally," he continued finally. "I mean she's the only woman I've ever been with—slept with. I always thought I was funny-looking, because when I was a kid girls laughed at me on account of I was so tall and thin. I guess I was funny-looking. Anyway, I never had the guts to make a pass at a girl—never in all my life."

The full implication of what he was saying began to sink in. Nature, in a final touch of irony, had picked an inhibited and sex-shy man to become the new father of his country. To some men the thought of possessing the entire female population as a private harem—even if most of the conception would be of necessity by remote control—would have been enormously satisfying to their ego. But to Homer it must have been sheer horror. It was this that had frightened him into his present decline, more than being jailed in the Shoreham's luxury, or being trotted around to Washington's most important salons, and placed on exhibition. "Go ahead and talk, Homer," I urged him.

"That's about all, except that I want Mary Ellen now more than I've ever wanted anything in all my life. I need her, Steve. I've got to have her!"

I thought to myself that if Homer's mother still lived it would be his mother, in all likelihood, whom he would want. I tried to remember what I had read about how an Œdipus complex is transferred. "They haven't let you see Mary Ellen?"

"Gosh, no. I begged them to let me go to Tarrytown for a day or two, or to let her come down here. Mrs. Brundidge could take care of the baby all right. But Colonel Phelps-Smythe and Mr. Klutz said absolutely not."

I wondered what was wrong with them, which shows how naive I was at the time. "Don't worry, Homer, I'll get it fixed up," I promised. For the first time, he smiled. He positively grinned. "Let's have another drink," I suggested, "and then tackle that dinner over there, and then let's go down to the Blue Room and look around."

"Sure!" he said. "Sure!"

He attacked the lobster as if he were starving, which I am quite sure he was, and ate most of the shrimp, and wolfed three of the pastries. I didn't do much talking. I kept trying to reconstruct the first ten years of his life in Hyannis, Nebraska. I saw a gangling kid, preyed upon by smaller but older boys, running to his mother for protection. I saw an overgrown high school sophomore teased by the girls, and not understanding that their teasing was as much invitation as anything else. I saw a lonesome youth escaping into archeology, and finally geology, who worked hard and earnestly so that in his mind there would be nothing else but his work. Finally I saw a grown man who had thrust human relationships into the well of his subconscious—a man whose marriage was probably the passionate seeking for a second mother to whom to run whenever he encountered the frightening facts of life.

This was the man chosen to re-populate the earth! I wasn't at all sure that I should arrange for him to see Mary Ellen. Perhaps he should see her for a day or two, but certainly he should not be with her constantly. A different therapy was indicated. "You know, Homer," I said, "what you told me about your personal life was very impressive. I suppose you know by now that you were mistaken. I should think you would be very attractive to women."

"Oh, no!" he said emphatically.

"I would think so."

"But why should I be?"

"Well, you're young, and you're tall. All the movie actors are tall. Look at Gary Cooper."

"Yes. But they're not so thin."

"Well, look at Frank Sinatra. Anyway, you've got a good frame. All you have to do is put some flesh on it."

Homer considered this. "I looked pretty good," he admitted, "when I was in Australia. Lots of fresh air, and exercise. I felt good, too, and ate well. I haven't had a bit of exercise since I've been in this darn prison."

"We'll fix that," I promised. "Now go shave, and put on a fresh shirt, and I'll take you out of this prison and show you how life is being lived, at the moment."

Ten seconds after we entered the Blue Room I discovered that acting as shepherd to Homer Adam would have complications, for Homer was no ordinary white sheep who could fade into the flock. If you are some six and one-half feet tall, and your hair flames like a stop light, and you are constructed on the general lines of a flagpole, and if in addition you are the most talked of mortal on earth, and your features are familiar to everyone who has seen a newspaper, then it is very hard to be inconspicuous.

When we turned up at the Blue Room and asked for a table, Pierre, the headwaiter, recognized Adam and almost did nip-ups. He bobbed us to a ringside table, swept away a notice that it was reserved, and then fluttered over our order for a couple of drinks. Barnee, the bandmaster, craned his neck, missed a beat, the trumpet went astray, and the rhythm scattered like a covey of quail. Nobody seemed to notice.

The band pulled itself together, and the music again took form. People were staring. If Homer had been a pink Bengal tiger, he could not have caused more of a sensation. I noticed that the dancing couples were converging towards us. Strangely, the women were maneuvering the men.

The music stopped, and there was absolute silence. Ordinarily, when the music isn't playing in a night spot it is still pretty noisy, what with the tinkle of glass and china, political and business arguments, the throaty sound of verbal lovemaking, and occasional laughter. But this time when the music stopped there was no sound at all. Then buzzing began, like a swarm of bees, but not exactly. It had a strange timbre to it. Finally I realized it was from three or four hundred women all whispering at once.

"What's wrong with these people?" Homer asked.

"I dunno," I evaded.

"This is worse than a dinner party. It makes me feel dizzy—all these people staring."

"Relax and drink your drink."

Homer obediently drank his drink. Across the floor I spotted Oscar Finney, who stepped out of a reporter's cocoon to become a Hollywood butterfly, officially titled Public Relations Counsellor, at a thousand a week. With him was a golden-skinned creature partially clad in gold lamé. I'm always forgetting names, but I never forget a shape like that. Once it belonged to Kitty Ruppe, who danced in the chorus line at an uptown club. Now its name had been changed to Kathy Riddell, and Oscar Finney had made it fairly famous as "The Frame." I say fairly famous, because Kathy Riddell was one of those Hollywood stars who never seems to appear in a movie, but you see her picture everywhere. She wasn't enough of an actress to make a USO troupe, but every young man would recognize her instantly, even from the rear, which is more than you can say for Cornell or Hayes.

Finney waved to me. I waved back. "These women," Homer said suddenly, "are giving me the creeps." I noticed that while the interest of many of the men had turned elsewhere than towards our table, every woman had her eyes fixed on Homer. Furthermore, they were being very womanly.

"What's wrong with them?" Homer asked.

"I think they want to have babies."

Homer's long neck stretched across the table, and his eyes grew round like a boy who has requested the facts of life from an elder brother. "Don't they—" he began. "I mean, are all the men—you know, isn't it possible—?" He stopped, thought for a moment, and went on: "What I mean to say is this, to be blunt. When you—we'll say you—when you go to bed—" He faltered again. "When you go to bed with your wife, what—I mean—"

"Oh, I see. Here's the way it is, Homer," I told him. "Everything is just as usual, except one thing. Afterwards, nothing happens. Nothing at all. No babies."

"Well, then why are these women—"

"It is a matter of instinct," I explained. "The instincts of man are purely physical, and of the moment. With women, it is different. Most women. I don't know about nymphomaniacs. But most women, essentially, want babies. Sure, babies are only part of it to women. But it is an essential part, where to the man it is no part at all. Get it?"

"Yes, I get it," said Homer, and sighed.

I looked up, and there was Oscar Finney, with The Frame. Her breasts looked round as radar globes, and she was tuning them on Homer. You can't chase old friends away from your table, and I did the introductions, but I told myself I wasn't having any more rye, because now was the time for all good men to be alert.

Kitty Ruppe, or Kathy Riddell, or The Frame—whatever you want to call her—was either a very smart girl (which at the time seemed doubtful) or she had been carefully coached. Anyway, apparently those radar globes told her something, because she began talking archeology. She had read in the papers how Homer intended being an archeologist, when he was young, and so there was a bond between them.

"Oh," said Homer, "are you interested in archeology?"

Indeed she was, The Frame replied. Had Homer ever heard of

Professor Ruppe, at the University of Chicago? Well, that was her father.

Homer hesitated, and then he said he thought the name sounded familiar, and wasn't he connected in some way with the Aztec excavations? Absolutely, said The Frame, and she herself was particularly interested in archeology in Mexico, and she was simply *fascinated* by the finds in the Temple of Huitzilopochtli. Homer said he was too.

It was quite the queerest supper club conversation I remember, but it only made me more suspicious. This plant smelled all the way to the top of the Washington Monument. No dope, he, my friend Oscar Finney. To hook the name of any actress to Homer Adam was worth how many columns? How many papers are there in the United States?

Presently I saw it was coming. It approached in the shape of one of those "house" photographers you will find in night clubs and places like the Blue Room. She wore a blue evening gown that matched the decor, and the camera she held in her hand, flash bulb attached, seemed incongruous as a debutante toting a forty-five. She asked us to move a little closer together. When she raised her camera I let my right arm slide around the back of The Frame's chair. Nobody noticed, except Finney. The flash came, the girl drifted away, and Finney said:

"Steve, you've got an evil and suspicious mind."

"Just careful," I said.

Homer and The Frame looked at us, not understanding, and then their conversation went back to Mexico. Oscar and I talked shop, and I fed Homer drinks. It was a necessary adjunct to my program of relaxation. You could almost see the layers of repression scale off his shoulders as the drinks took hold, and his interest mounted in The Frame—or her archeology. Two tables away I saw Senator Fay Sumner Knott. She had been sitting there all the time, but I did not notice her until she began to move, in the same way that a snake seems part of the ground until it bunches itself to strike.

Of course you know Senator Knott. When she was nineteen she was the most beautiful debutante in New York, when she was twenty-five she was the loveliest young matron in London, and at thirty she was the smartest divorcée in Rhode Island, both in brains and looks. When she was thirty-five she married the President of Executive Trust, thereby becoming the most beautiful, the brainiest, and almost the richest woman in the world. At least, that was her opinion. When Executive Trust died she dipped a dainty toe into the mud puddle of politics, and lo, there she was in the Senate.

Fay kept looking at Homer, but Homer kept his eyes on The Frame. Presently Fay rose and walked past our table, slim and magic as a wand, but holding her chin tip-tilted to erase the lines in her neck. She ignored The Frame as if her chair were vacant, smiled at Homer, nodded at me, and just at the proper distance—close enough so that we could hear but it would not be heard at other tables— said: "That stupid little bitch!"

The Frame started out of her chair like a leopardess, but Oscar grabbed her, and anyway Fay had already reached the door. I knew she was trouble—big trouble. Homer was white, and his bony hands were shaking. Oscar said: "What a pleasant job you've got, Steve! What a nice, uncomplicated, pleasant job!"

Wasn't it, I agreed. I signed the check, herded Homer to an elevator, and led him to his bedroom in the distinguished guest suite. I helped him undress, fed him a couple of aspirins, made him drink two glasses of carbonated water, and rolled him into bed. His feet stuck a half-foot over the end, but there was nothing I could do about it.

CHAPTER 6

Before I opened my eyes, the next morning, I could smell coffee, and for some time there seemed no doubt that I was in Smith Field, and that Marge had wakened me first. I didn't hear coffee bubbling, however, nor did I hear the radio, nor did Marge tickle me behind the ears, the way she usually did when it was time to get up. I just smelled coffee. I opened my eyes and discovered that I was in the Adam suite, but that something new had been added.

I won't describe her the way she first appeared to me, because that would be unfair. I will describe her the way she was, and is. Jane Zitter, in her way, is a wonderful girl. Wonderful. It is true that she is not beautiful, in the sense that The Frame is beautiful, or Fay Sumner Knott is beautiful, or Marge is beautiful. She has something beyond regular features, a perfect complexion, or streamlined legs. Jane Zitter is part of the workaday world. She is as much a part as a freighter that carries its seven thousand tons of grain at a steady eight knots. No glamour, just service.

She is a little person all around. She isn't very tall, and she isn't filled out in the right places. About the best you can say for her clothes is that they are neat, and her thick glasses make her eyes larger and rounder than they actually are, so that she appears perpetually startled.

She'll never get to be a secretary to a Secretary to the President. She is simply a lubricant for the wheels of government. When the oil becomes gritty with age it is changed, and nobody knows what happens to the old and cracked and tired oil. All that matters is that the wheels still turn.

I opened my eyes and Jane shoved a cup of coffee at me, black. "I suppose you wonder who I am," she began.

"Oh, no! Not at all! I expect to wake up with strange females in my bedroom."

"Mr. Smith, I hope I didn't make a mistake. I'm your secretary. My name is Jane Zitter and I'm your secretary and everything was piling up so that I thought it best that if Mr. Smith wouldn't go to the office then the office had better go to Mr. Smith."

I told her I thought this was very nice of the office, and it was an arrangement of which I approved, particularly if the office appeared with black coffee. "But I really don't see why I have to have an office at all," I added. "You see, I'm not a real executive of N.R.P. I'm just a sort of glorified nurse-maid."

Jane turned her startled eyes on my red pajamas. "But if you didn't have an office, how would you answer your mail, and your telegrams, and dictate your memoranda?"

"I'm not going to dictate any memoranda," I said firmly. "Not a one."

"But you have to dictate memoranda," Jane said. "People write you memoranda, and you have to write them back. Why, already you've received a whole envelope full, and I've got them with me, in case you care to work here. You see, you're quite an important man, Mr. Smith, being Special Assistant to the Director, and so you get copies of all the really important memoranda that originate in National Re-fertilization, plus the important inter-office and inter-departmental memos, even those classified secret and top secret."

I could see she was genuinely serious, and so I decided to be serious too because I didn't want my secretary to have any delusions that I was a Klutz, or even a half-Klutz. "Look, Miss Zitter," I said, pushing myself up in bed, "under no circumstances—not ever—will I write a memorandum to anyone about anything. That is a pledge. May God strike me dead if I do!"

"Oh, Mr. Smith—"

"Never, so help me Christ!"

"But you don't understand, Mr. Smith. If you don't answer the memoranda, or at least initial them, the files would never get cleared! You see, here's the way it works. Suppose Mr. Klutz sent you a memo."

"God forbid!"

Jane went on persistently and patiently. "Well, suppose Mr. Klutz sent a memo to Mr. Gableman, for action, with copies to you and the other members of the Planning Board for information. Well, until everybody has done something about that memo, it hasn't been cleared up or settled, and the file clerks cannot put it in the files."

"It floats around in a kind of limbo?"

"Yes, exactly."

"Unless I initial a memo it can never die?"

"It can never die, Mr. Smith. It just keeps coming back to you and coming back to you from the communications section, and they write covering memos to you calling your attention to the first memo, and so on, and this complicates things. Please, Mr. Smith, I hope you will do something about this, because if you don't people will think I'm inefficient, and I'll get some kind of bad report on my 201 file, and I'll never be able to get my classification changed."

She appeared solemn, and a bit pitiful, and she was obviously such a nice girl. "I'll make a deal," I said. "You learn to make my initials, and you initial every memo that comes to the office. That's all you have to do."

"Won't you ever read any of them?"

"Never!"

"Well, certainly you'll read some of the directives. Everybody reads the directives, because they're classified secret."

"Never!"

Jane Zitter shook her head. "Oh, dear, Mr. Smith, the N.R.P. is such a strange organization, and you are such a strange man! Sometimes I think I should never have left Interior. I get six hundred more with N.R.P. than I did with Interior, and I thought working with N.R.P. would be more progressive, and advanced, and even exciting. But I never thought it would be anything like this." She looked again at my red pajamas. "I suppose you're crazy," she reflected, "and I'll probably get into trouble, but I won't let you down."

I remembered Homer, in his bedroom down the hall, and wondered whether I'd fed him enough drinks to afflict him with a hangover. Jane seemed to anticipate my question. "Mr. Adam," she said, "went out."

"Went out?"

"Oh, yes. He went out an hour ago. I told him I didn't know whether he should or not, but he said you had said he could do anything he pleased. And out he went."

"Did he say where?"

"He said somebody had called and he had made an engagement to discuss archeology. He didn't say where or with whom. He just said, 'I'm going to see a person about archeology.' He appeared very happy about it, and chipper. He even tried to comb his hair."

"Oh, my," I said. "He's been kidnaped by The Frame!"

"The Frame!"

I scrambled out of bed. "Either turn your head or go into the next room," I told Jane. "We've got to find out what this is all about."

She apparently didn't think I was especially dangerous, because she simply turned her head.

I dressed in a hurry, although I wasn't actually worried. As a matter of fact, the thought of Homer being interested in The Frame was in some ways encouraging. At least one inhibition was breaking down, and for a man in Homer's position, such an inhibition was not good for the soul. Further, it seemed a good sign that his lethargy and despondency could be cured. He could go out with The Frame if he wanted—so long as complications didn't develop. However, I wasn't going to allow any Hollywood press agent to use Homer for creating headlines. If Homer found relaxation and a measure of escape with The Frame, it was one thing. But as a publicity stunt, it was out.

I called the Press Club, located Finney, and got him on the phone. "Look, Oscar," I said, "that bimbo of yours is out with my boy Homer, and it smells ungood."

"Oh, is that where she went?" Oscar said. "I've been trying to reach her all morning, because I'm going to New York."

"You know damn well that's where she is," I said.

"No. Honest, Steve, I didn't." He sounded like he was telling the truth.

"Oscar," I warned him, "don't try to pull any stunts with Adam. This business is too fundamental to mess it up just for the sake of a little publicity."

Finney hesitated a moment before he answered. Finally he said, "Steve, I'll lay it on the line. Kathy herself suggested it would be a smart pitch to hook her up with Adam. She's been after me about it for days. Last night when I saw you and Adam in the Blue Room I thought I'd go ahead with it. Then I thought, no, I'd better not. For one thing, from now on Kathy's got to make her name on the screen, and not in the papers. And it might have bad repercussions, especially with the women. She's not too popular with the women now, for a number of obvious reasons, and if it looked as if she were trying to snag the only whole male on earth, she might get decidedly unpopular. You saw how that amateur Borgia acted last night. I told Riddell to lay off. I told her that grabbing Adam would be like stealing the U.S. Mint, and it would be bad box office. So she said okay, and if she's out with Adam, then it's news to me. Do you know where they are?"

"Haven't the foggiest notion," I said, and added, "Don't get me wrong. I don't mind Homer seeing Kitty—or Kathy—so long as it doesn't break into print. It might be good for Homer."

"Have you ever seen a pregnant starlet?" Oscar inquired.

"Don't worry," I reassured him, "Homer is shy and harmless. Nothing like that is going to happen."

"Riddell isn't harmless," Oscar said. "Furthermore, she might get ideas. All the women seem to be crazy nowadays. There are plenty of girls out on the Coast who wouldn't think of spoiling their figures by having babies when babies could be begat by their own husbands with no trouble at all. Now that they can't have 'em, they all want 'em."

I told Oscar I would be responsible. It occurred to me that for a newspaperman who had always watched other people carrying the world's burdens I was making myself responsible for a lot of things.

It wasn't hard to locate Adam and The Frame, for as I pointed out he was not a person who could vanish into the stream of humanity without a ripple. The doorman at the Shoreham remembered that Mr. Adam had taken a cab to the Smithsonian Institute. Jane wondered why, and I told her about the archeological mating of Homer and The Frame.

At the Smithsonian we went to the South American annex. It was a good guess. We found Homer and the girl sitting on a stone bench, her tawny hair barely brushing his shoulder, staring steadfastly at what appeared to be a large and ornately carved stone altar.

Behind them, glaring from the wall, was a horrid wooden mask, with tusks, which could frighten large adults.

I will say this for The Frame. She not only had a shape on which to hang clothes, but apparently she possessed an instinct for what clothes to hang on the shape. Now she looked as if she had just been voted the Best Dressed Senior in her college. I don't recall exactly what she wore, except that it was something with a wide belt and a flaring skirt, and it gave her that collegiate look which blends so well with an interest in archeology.

"Hello, people," I greeted them. "If you want to be alone I can think of more comfy places, without goons like that." I nodded at the mask.

They didn't appear particularly happy to see us. "I hope you don't mind, Steve," Homer protested. "You're not going to be a Phelps-Smythe, are you? You said I could do whatever I wanted, you know."

"Of course, Homer," I soothed him, "but just let me know what's going on. If you start wandering off, and I don't know where you are, people might not understand. First thing you know you'll find yourself being tailed by the FBI and the Secret Service and Army G-2, and maybe Abel Pumphrey himself—it would frighten him so."

"We were followed," said The Frame. "I'm sure of it."

"Honest?"

"Absolutely," said Homer.

"By who?"

"I don't know. Kathy noticed him first. I never got a good look at him. But he's somewhere in the building now."

"Don't worry," I said. "I'll find out about it. So long as you don't get in a jam, what the hell? People can't object to you taking an interest in some old stones or mummy cases."

Jane Zitter looked worried. "That might depend," she observed, "as to who's acting as guide." I noticed that Jane and The Frame were eyeing each other like a pair of strange tabbies, and remembered the introductions. Then I asked, casually:

"And how is archeology today?"

"We were just discussing the legend of Tezcatlipoca," The Frame remarked coolly. "Although one cannot really call it a legend, since it has been so well authenticated."

"It must be fascinating."

"It is for poor Homer," said The Frame, "because he can see himself in it."

Homer's lips smiled, but his eyes were sad as a spaniel's. "That is quite true," he said, and explained.

It seems that one of the most bizarre Aztec rites was in honor of the god Tezcatlipoca, the god of fertility and creation. He was depicted as a young man, and handsome. Once each year the Aztecs picked a young man to represent the god. For a year he lived in splendor, and led the most exotic kind of life. His clothes were the finest, he was sprinkled daily with perfume, and flowers were thrown in his path when he went abroad. He was attended by the royal pages, and the people prostrated themselves when they saw him.

Four beautiful girls, each bearing the name of a goddess—or more if he wanted them—were his.

Things went along like this for a year, but at the end of a year they took him to the top of their highest pyramid, and stretched him naked on a sacrificial stone of jasper. "Just like this one," Homer said.

Then a red-robed priest zipped open his chest and cut out his heart with a volcanic stone knife, holding it aloft towards the sun. The corpse was thrown to the foot of the pyramid. "And then," Homer continued, shuddering, "they ate him!"

"I would not worry too much about that last part," I told him. "They might find some soup bones on you, but I don't see any steaks."

The Frame leaned against Homer. "I think he is perfectly fine as he is," she said. "You are just trying to fatten him up so you can use him for your own purposes—all of you."

"Miss Riddell," I asked, "are you against A.I.?"

"Theoretically, no," replied The Frame. "I suppose the human race must be perpetuated, although sometimes"—she glanced at Jane Zitter—"I don't see why. But I don't think we are going about it properly, nor do I believe proper consideration is given to Homer's feelings."

"I know things aren't perfect," I admitted. "Naturally Homer suffers some inconvenience. But can you think of a better way than A.I. to accomplish our purpose?"

"I certainly can!" The Frame said defiantly.

I said we'd talk it over again sometime, and I told Homer I'd see him at dinner, and Jane and I left them to whatever it was they found in the South American annex.

That afternoon Jane persuaded me to go to my office while she initialed memos. It was quite an office I had, as a Special Assistant to the Director of N.R.P., and I was surprised to find that in the really few hours I had been in Washington it was already filling up with letters and telegrams. While Jane did her paperwork, I read a few of them.

There was a letter from Senator Frogham. He congratulated me on my appointment, and hoped he could be of service when a bill for continuing N.R.P. came to the Senate floor—a gentle hint that N.R.P. could not continue forever by presidential order alone.

He went on to say that many of his constituents had written concerning the possibility of bearing an Adam child, and he felt the needs of his state should be considered when the question of first priorities arose.

There was a long, carefully composed, registered letter from the president of the National Insurance Council. He started by saying that the country was on disaster's brink. People were not buying new insurance policies, because as things presently stood, the future of their progeny was uncertain. If this kept up, thousands of salesmen would be thrown out of work, the companies themselves might collapse, there would be inflation, depression, and the insurance business generally would go to hell. In that case, the country was doomed.

The answer, he said, obviously was to take the sound view that Adam's children be allotted to people willing to insure the future of those children—the holders of insurance policies. Furthermore, any family which applied for the seed of Adam should be forced to take out policies on whatever children Adam's seed produced. Thus could disaster be averted.

There was a telegram from the U.S. Chamber of Commerce, urging that an optimistic note be given to official releases on the health and well-being of Mr. Adam. Whenever rumors spread that Mr. Adam was ill, or that there was friction within N.R.P., or that Mr. Adam had been found unsuitable for A.I.—and naturally such rumors kept cropping up—securities collapsed. The Chamber of Commerce felt that above all, everybody should be optimistic.

Both the C.I.O. and the A.F. of L. sent notes that they were confident the rights of feminine union members would be protected when the time came for A.I. to commence. Otherwise, there would be very real and concrete danger of a wholly capitalistic world.

There was a letter from a Hellenic society pointing out that Greece's population had been greatly reduced by war casualties, out-lining Greece's long record of service to mankind, and requesting priority for Greece when the rights of small nations came under consideration. There was the same type of request from the Poles, the Moslem League, the Armenians, and the Daughters of the American Revolution.

It appeared that there was hardly a group of any kind in all the world—and certainly none which maintained offices in Washington—which couldn't present a good argument for special attention from the N.R.P. I realized I had become a target, albeit a moving target, for lobbyists and pressure groups. The announcement of my appointment automatically set me up as a clay pigeon. The question of allotting the seed of Adam was one I decided to duck.

Jane Zitter, who had been bulldozing her way through pink,

green, and red piles of paper on her desk, suddenly lifted her head and said, "She's up to something. I can't figure it out."

"Who?"

"That girl—The Frame. She's clever."

"Sure she's clever," I admitted. "But it's perfectly obvious what she wants. She wants Homer Adam. But then, so does everybody else, and most of them are pretty damn selfish. You can tell by reading my mail. You've got to hand it to The Frame. She goes out to get him, personally. She doesn't write letters explaining why she, and no other woman, is entitled to first crack at Homer. She has drive, and initiative."

Jane shook her head. "No, I think you're wrong. I suspect her of everything. She might even be a Communist agent. Hollywood is full of Communists, isn't it?"

"I don't know," I said. "I always thought Washington was full of Commies. For all I know you might be a Communist."

"She's an actress," Jane said. "She's playing a part. She practically ambushes Mr. Adam in the Blue Room, and then she attacks him on his only vulnerable front, which is archeology. It is too perfect."

"I would not worry," I said. "Homer has a perfectly good wife in Tarrytown, and only yesterday he was begging me to let him see her."

"He won't beg any more," Jane predicted.

As the days went by, it turned out she was correct. Homer didn't mention Mary Ellen again. He took The Frame to the Aztec Gardens in the Pan-American Union, and they spent hours deep under the stacks of the Library of Congress, and in the basement of the Archives Building, and in the gloomy reading rooms of the Pan-Hispanic Library. On the surface it all looked like good, wholesome, scholarly companionship, but this seemed hardly believable.

Whatever it was, I did not try to discourage it, for Homer visibly blossomed. His face no longer resembled that of a fresh-dug cadaver,

and in a week he gained eight pounds, although when you distrib-
uted eight pounds up and down the length of his frame it did not
seem very much.

While they spent their days in the pursuit of Aztec culture,
that wasn't the way they spent their evenings. They went out together every night, and each night Homer faithfully told me where
they were going. It was always the Footlight Club, a little place on
Connecticut Avenue where the steaks weren't bad, the drinks cheap,
and you could dance to a five-piece band. Of this I approved. I didn't
want him trotting The Frame around to any of the big places where
they'd be conspicuous and get their names in the papers.

But one evening Homer came home more mussed than usual.
Ordinarily we played a couple of games of gin before we turned in,
but this night Homer played two hands as if he had been knocked
on the head. Then he got up from the table and poured himself a
drink. He turned to me and said, "Kathy is going back to Hollywood tomorrow."

"That's too bad," I said. "I think she's been good for you."

He ran a hand through his hair, and I could see that he was
trembling. This was not encouraging. I thought he was finished with
the shakes. "Steve," he said, "is it possible for a man to be in love
with two women at the same time?"

"It has been done," I said.

"I think I am in love with Kathy."

When a man says he is in love with a woman there is nothing
you can tell him, except to congratulate him, and it did not seem
that Homer should be congratulated, considering the circumstances.
I kept quiet.

"I suppose I love Mary Ellen, too," he went on. "At least I ought
to. She is my wife and until tonight I always thought I loved her very
much. But I'm not sure that I love Mary Ellen the way I love Kathy."

"No?"

"No. I think Mary Ellen and I got married because we were both a little lonesome. We were two strays wandering around in a world where everyone else was paired off. But with Kathy it is different. We were made for each other. It isn't only archeology."

"It is rarely archeology."

Homer began to pace up and down. "It isn't only archeology," he repeated. "It is everything. We were made for each other."

"Now what gave you that idea?"

"Kathy told me. We didn't go to the Footlight Club tonight. We went up to Kathy's room in her hotel."

"Pardon me a moment," I said. I went into the bathroom, shut the door, and banged my head against the wall. I came out again and asked Homer to tell me exactly how far things had gone, and what happened, in detail. He stammered, and cracked his knuckles, and got red in the face, and finally said that things had gone as far as they could go, but that it wasn't his fault.

"Now, look, Homer," I said, "you weren't raped, were you?"

"Well, not exactly," he said. "I'm not sure. Nothing like that ever happened to me before. One minute we were discussing the Toltecs, and the next minute we had all our clothes off."

I said the fatuous thing that mothers tell their daughters and fathers their sons and husbands tell their wives: "Homer, this sounds like a mere infatuation."

"Perhaps," Homer said miserably. "I don't know. I'm all mixed up."

I shoved Homer into a chair, sat down opposite him, put my hands on his shoulders, and glared into his eyes like an optometrist. "Homer," I said, "you are not going to like what I have to say, but I must tell it to you."

"Go ahead."

"Homer, you are one of those rare men chosen for real sacrifice to the world. You are a fine man, Homer, and certainly no one can blame you for your personal feelings. But it is your destiny to be sacrificed, like that Aztec god, what's his name—"

"Tezcatlipoca," Homer provided.

"No man has ever been sacrificed for so great a cause," I continued. "Homer, first you must do your duty to mankind, and then remember your wife and little Eleanor. After that, you can think of The Frame—Kathy. I hardly need to tell you what the repercussions would be if your affair with Kathy became public."

"You don't have to tell me," Homer said. "I know. That's what I don't understand. Kathy doesn't seem to appreciate my position. She wanted me to run away with her."

"Wanted you to run away! Where?"

"She didn't say. Just away. It scared me. I told her I couldn't do it—that I had my obligations, and she said to think it over, and that obviously we were destined to be together always, and that when I decided I should call her."

"And you said?"

"I said I would think it over."

I began to breathe again. "Thank goodness, Homer, you are being sensible. You have done a very noble thing, and it is a shame it will forever be hidden from history."

That night I lay awake thinking. I really felt very solemn about it. Plenty of men would have told the world to take a flying leap at a galloping goose, and would have proceeded to do their own re-fertilization in their own way. But Homer was a very decent, public-spirited citizen. On the other hand I didn't quite understand The Frame's procedure. She was a smart girl—smart enough to know that she couldn't possibly get away with eloping with Homer permanently. Or could she, say, if they got out of the country? The thought worried me.

I decided that the best way for Homer to keep his balance, and forget about The Frame, was to bring Mary Ellen to Washington. I was afraid that as soon as The Frame left, Homer would start pining away again, and sink into his melancholia.

In the morning I went into Homer's room and found he was dressing. "Where are you going?" I asked.

"I'm seeing Kathy off. She's catching the noon plane for Los Angeles."

"Homer," I said, "I don't think that is wise. Why prolong the agony? You'll just make it tough on yourself. You've made your decision, now stick with it."

Homer sat down on the bed, his bare, lathlike legs almost touching his chin, and put his head in his hands. "I just wanted to see her this once more," he said. "Just this one more time."

I felt like saying to hell with it, and taking him down to the airport and putting him on the Coast plane, then I remembered Marge, and how anxious she was that something come of this business, and all the other women who were really sincerely troubled, and what a mess the world would be in if Homer ran off with The Frame. "It would be bad, Homer," I said. "It would be especially bad since I'm arranging for Mary Ellen to come to Washington and stay here with you, at least until A.I. begins. See what I mean?"

"Yes," he said, "I see."

"You do want to see Mary Ellen, don't you?"

"Why of course I want to see her. I'm all confused."

"Naturally you're confused. All of us get confused once in a while. You've just had more than your share in a short space of time."

Homer groaned.

"Since you'll probably see Mary Ellen tonight, it would only make it worse to see Kathy at noon, wouldn't it?"

"I suppose so, but I promised Kathy—"

I put my hand on his shoulder, feeling more or less like a heel. "You don't worry about that," I said. "I'll go to the airport and see her off, and tell her how things are. I'll take the responsibility."

"Will you?" Homer said gratefully. "Thanks, Steve." He hesitated a moment and then asked: "Steve, what shall I tell Mary Ellen?"

"Tell her? Why tell her nothing! Not a word! Not a hint!"

"But that seems unfair."

"Homer, believe me, if there is one thing a woman would rather not hear about a thing like that, it is the truth. If it ever comes up, deny everything. That's an order!"

"But—"

"Homer, about this there can be no buts. If you want to lead a life of utter and complete misery, just start confessing. But as long as you are married to Mary Ellen and it looks like your marriage is going to last, lie, lie, lie until your teeth drop out!"

Homer looked at me in shock and wonder, like a Boy Scout whose Scoutmaster has uttered a bad word, but he nodded yes. However, when I left for National Airport, I still had misgivings.

The wind was playing hide-and-seek around the ramp at the airport, and it was an unseasonably warm day. The Frame was carrying her fur coat across her arm, and the wind had shellacked her dress against her, outlining a sight that could cast men into a trance. "Hello, Steve," she said, smiling at my stares, "where's Homer?"

"He's not seeing you any more," I said. "His wife is coming down from New York right away."

"Did he tell you about us?"

"Yes."

"Everything?"

"Yes."

She wasn't smiling any more. Her chin was set and her eyes, tawny, golden-brown eyes which men forgot to notice, were steady. "Steve," she said, "you remember me when I was a kid in New York, club-dancing, don't you?"

"Sure."

"I suppose you thought I was a brainless little tramp. Well, Steve, all kids are a little wild when they first go to New York. I got over that. This isn't simply an infatuation."

"It has got to be simply an infatuation," I said. "There are things you've forgotten. There's his wife and daughter, and there's A.I."

"Your foolish A.I.!" she said. She had the strangest expression on her face. Some evangelists get it, and you used to see it in the pictures of Nazis while they listened to Hitler, and madmen wear it. It is fanaticism, and it is always frightening.

The loudspeakers were calling her flight. "Well, happy landings, Kathy," I said. "But I might as well be frank. I don't see any hope for it."

"You don't? Well, you try to stop me, Steve! You can't turn destiny aside, or halt the will of God."

Everyone on the ramp stared when she boarded the plane. I knew what they all were thinking. But as for me, she only made me shiver. You think you know a lot about a person, and then you find out you don't know anything about what goes on inside. I realized that Kitty Ruppe was much too complicated a bit of feminine machinery for me to piece together all by myself. On the way back to the Shoreham I stopped off at the FBI.

CHAPTER 7

Mary Ellen arrived the next day. I had forgotten what an attractive girl she was, in a healthy Midwest way, and perhaps Homer had, too, because he seemed genuinely glad to see her. For a while I followed them about like an unwelcome duenna, fearful that Homer would implicate himself with The Frame by a thoughtless remark, but he appeared more self-possessed than at any time since he had been installed in Washington.

Mary Ellen was one of the few women I've ever seen who looks good with a shiny nose. She was fresh and crisp as newly laundered linen, and she had a lot of bounce. Things rocked along nicely, but the very sight of Mary Ellen and Homer holding hands and behaving like they were on a honeymoon made me feel lonesome and dispirited. On Sunday morning I put Jane Zitter in charge of the menage Adam and flew to New York. I soothed my conscience by telling myself I was duty bound to see Thompson and Ostenheimer, and give them a report on Adam's progress.

My home, and my wife, made Washington feel unreal and faraway. Marge was wearing a new dress when I arrived, one of those dresses that make you keep watching. She was all smelled up with perfume, and it seemed to me that her makeup was a bit too perfect, and her hair-do a little professional. "You think we're going out to-night," I accused her, "but we're not."

She kissed me experimentally. "Of course not, darling," she said. "We're going to stay right here, and Maria and Tommy Thompson are coming over, and we'll play bridge and talk." She kissed me again, as if she were testing my breath for liquor, or something.

"What's wrong with you?" I asked.

"Is there anything wrong with me wanting to kiss you?"

"No, certainly not. I like it. That's why I'm here."

"You've been having fun in Washington, haven't you dear?"

"Fun? Hell no. What a snafu."

"Your face is all full of lipstick," she said. She took a handkerchief and went to work on me. "I thought it would be fun for you, with that curvy wench—what's her name—The Frame?"

"The Frame! What about me and The Frame?"

"Oh, nothing. I just saw a picture of you and what's her name— The Frame—in the *Journal-American*. The caption said something about Mr. Adam, glimpsed with the Special Assistant to the Director of N.R.P., the former newspaperman Stephen Decatur Smith, and The Frame, at a fashionable supper club. Since you had your arm around The Frame, I thought you must be having fun."

This is the kind of reward people get for trying to render a public service. About a matter like this there is no use being serious. The more earnest your pleas of innocence, the more guilty you seem. I said, "That's what you get for reading the *Journal-American*."

"She must be charming," Marge said. "And she's probably very much impressed with your official position. I really don't see why you bothered to come to New York and visit me, except of course you probably have business to discuss with Maria and Dr. Thompson."

"Of course I've got business to discuss with them," I said, "and of course that's the only reason I came to New York. As a matter of fact, I do not see how I can stay the night."

Marge kissed me again, and this time it wasn't testing. "Come on," she said, "give." I told her about Homer and The Frame. It made her very thoughtful. "Stephen," she said, "I think you're in trouble. If that girl gets Homer, where will that leave the rest of us?"

"But she's not going to get Homer. His wife is with him now, and they seem perfectly happy and contented."

"But that isn't much better."

I considered this a very queer statement. "Marge," I inquired, "honestly, are you considering having a baby by A.I.?"

"Perhaps," she said. I knew that meant yes. Instantly, I felt betrayed. I felt like a cuckold, and I knew that every other husband whose wife contemplated having an A.I. baby would feel the same. I know it wasn't sensible, but there it was, as fundamental as Homer's desire for The Frame, or Marge's urge to have children.

When Tommy Thompson and Maria arrived they seemed to be tiptoeing on a pink cloud. His St. Bernard eyes followed her, proud and possessive and devoted, and she sat beside him, and squirmed against his shoulder. A love affair between two doctors, or between a doctor and a nurse, is sometimes difficult to understand. How they can reconcile the terms of medical anatomy with the delicate language of passion is something that has never been fully explained, but they do it all the time.

Of course we talked about A.I. We played bridge, in the sense that someone dealt cards and we looked at them, but mostly we talked. Except Tommy didn't talk much. Tommy Thompson was thinking. He did his thinking slowly. When you watched him you could almost hear his brain go click, click, click like an old grandfather clock, just as creaky, and just as right.

"I'll tell you," he said finally, "I don't think the world is going to be permanently sterile. I think there's a chance for it."

"You mean through Mr. Adam?" Marge asked.

"Perhaps. He might get it started."

"What then?"

"Well," Tommy hesitantly explained, "you know I've been experimenting. I'm not entirely satisfied that the male sperm is really dead. I think he is stunned, knocked out, paralyzed, but I'm not sure he is dead. I think I saw one wriggle."

"When you look through a microscope too long everything wriggles," said Maria.

"No, I am sure I saw one wriggle." Tommy looked into his glass, as if he saw one there. "I might as well tell you all about it. I've been working eighteen hours a day on this idea of mine. If it is true that the male germ isn't totally destroyed, then it is just a matter of nursing him back—or jarring him back—into full vitality. I've got a compound—"

"Quack!" I interrupted. "Medicine man! Purveyor of snake oil!"

"It is a silly sort of business," he continued, ignoring me. "It is mostly seaweed. High iodized content."

"That's very interesting," said Maria, suddenly alert. "Why don't you try it out?"

"I am trying it out. But I need more experimental animals—mostly husbands. How about you, Steve? Some of my colleagues at Polyclinic are taking it."

"Not me," I said. "I'm no guinea pig."

Marge looked at me. "Go ahead and try it," she urged. "You ought to contribute something to humanity."

"All over the world," I replied, "pathologists and biologists and endocrinologists are undoubtedly working, just like Tommy here, on such ideas. Maybe Tommy or one of the others will come up with something. When he does, why naturally I'll take it. But right at the moment I don't feel like filling my stomach with seaweed."

"You're a big help!" said Marge. "You're practically a traitor to the human race!"

"If he changes his mind," Tommy told her, "I'll give him a bottle of the stuff. It can't hurt him—at least I don't think it can hurt him because it hasn't hurt any of the others. I prescribe forty drops a day, in this test period, and none of the fellows at the hospital are sick yet. On the other hand none of them seem to be starting any babies."

"He won't change his mind," Marge said. "He just doesn't want to have any children—never has."

I didn't argue. What was the sense of arguing? Marge has that damnable type of memory that goes back through the years and picks up evidence that you have long forgotten, and drowns you in it.

I told Maria and Tommy about Homer's progress, touching lightly on the episode of The Frame, and they agreed that it sounded as if he were greatly improved, and probably on the way to recovery. They promised to come down to Washington and look him over. Perhaps he was in shape for the beginning of A.I., although they couldn't be sure until they'd given him a thorough checkup.

At nine o'clock we listened to Winchell. He sounded breathless as if he had run up twenty flights in Radio City. He started off with a flash from London. The British Foreign Office had learned, he said, that two unsterilized males had been discovered in Outer Mongolia. They had been discovered several months ago, but the Russians were keeping it a secret. It seems that they were miners, and like Adam they had been in the lowest level of a deep lead workings when Mississippi blew up.

"That's very interesting," Tommy said. "I wonder if it's true?"

"It sounds plausible," said Maria.

"I don't think so," I said. "It isn't very likely that the British Foreign Office would know what goes on in Outer Mongolia. There probably have been some rumors floating around, and finally the rumors reached London, and the Foreign Office allowed them to leak, just to sound out the Russians as to whether they were true."

"If it is true, what effect would that have on the N.R.P.?" Marge asked.

"Oh, I think it would start a production race between us and the Russians. And there would be a lot of pressure to utilize Adam immediately. I'm glad he's better, because even the hint of an unsterilized Russian is likely to send Washington spinning."

"It is sort of frightening," Marge said. "Those Mongols breed like mice, don't they?"

"All things considered," Tommy said, "I think a good husky Mongol would outbreed Adam three to one, from what I have seen of him."

"That's probably true," said Maria, "but if we're able to perfect improved methods of A.I. utilizing a single germ for each impregnation—which as you know is what I've been working on—why we can meet their competition. However, they're just as advanced as we are in those things and if they have two men to our one, and a bigger population to work with, why I suppose they can keep their birth rate well above ours."

I said it was all hypothetical anyway, until something definite was known, and if it was true then that was good, because then both countries would get together and pool their knowledge and perhaps save the human race after all. Maria said she didn't think it would work out that way, because all her experiments were viewed as military secrets, and she supposed it was the same with the Russians.

I explained about military secrets, so far as I knew. It seems that every major power has two operations, one called S.I.—Secret Intelligence—and the other C.I.—Counter Intelligence. "Now that this is peacetime," I said, "ordinarily those guys would be back in their normal occupations as purveyors of buggy whips, peddlers of brushes, operators of shooting galleries, and clam and oyster salesmen. But a secret agent makes a lot of money and he doesn't have to account for it. In every country in the world it is called 'unvouchered funds,' and a secret agent supposedly pays out these unvouchered funds to people for information."

"It sounds very profitable," Marge agreed.

"Oh, it is. It is a wonderful racket. It is sort of an international club. All the fellows in S.I. try to penetrate other countries, and all the fellows in C.I. try to keep other countries from penetrating us."

"We have very nice counter-intelligence men," Maria objected. "They come to see me all the time. They put up baskets in our laboratories, and we are supposed to throw all our notes in them, and then they come around and burn the baskets. It is just like collecting the garbage, only cleaner."

"Is that all they do?" asked Marge.

"Oh, no. They make you sign papers."

"The British," I explained, "are wise to the racket, and they do it better. Most of the men in the British Secret Service have to hold other jobs too. In that way the government gets some work out of them. It is also a very good cover, because it is an honest cover. We aren't that smart. A guy turns up in a place like Istanbul and claims to be a reporter for *Field and Stream*, or *Vogue*, and everyone knows it is a phoney cover, but nobody says anything about it, because it would hurt the racket generally."

The telephone rang. It was Jane, in Washington. The N.R.P. was boiling, she said. Everybody was excited about the news from Outer Mongolia. Both Gableman and Mr. Pumphrey had called, and they wanted me to return to Washington immediately. There was to be a special conference with the State Department at ten in the morning, and the Planning Board would meet at eleven, and at noon Mr. Pumphrey would call at the White House. "But is it true about this Outer Mongolian business?" I asked.

"They don't know," Jane said. "But whether it is true or not, it is bound to have repercussions in Congress, and that's what worries them."

"Nothing doing," I said. "Tell them I've got a very important business engagement with the Advisory Committee, and we are discussing every phase of the situation. Tell them I'll bring in the recommendations of the Advisory Committee when I get back. Do you think that will fix it?"

"I hope so," Jane said, "but they are terribly excited."

She asked how soon I'd be back, and I said probably in a couple of days, unless something really urgent developed. She said that was all right, and she would call Mr. Gableman and Mr. Pumphrey and stress the importance of my conferring with the medical advisers at this time. I said she was a sweetheart, and that I would give her a kiss when I got back, because I saw that Marge was listening.

"You don't make me a bit jealous," Marge said when I hung up. "That was your secretary, and she doesn't worry me at all, if you gave me an accurate description of her. However, I'm still not sure about that Hollywood person."

Maria and Tommy left about one. Smith Field never seemed so wonderful.

When I awoke, sleet and rain were beating against our windows. Marge was scratching me behind the ears, and I relaxed with the luxurious determination to spend the day in bed and thumb my nose at the weather, Washington, the N.R.P., A.I., and unsterilized Mongolians.

All our lives, most of us have been the targets of a devilish propaganda campaign designed to rout us out of bed at the same hour as the beasts of the field and the farmyard. Whoever invented the slogan "Early to bed and early to rise makes a man healthy, wealthy, and wise," was an advertising genius. That slogan bullies most of us from childhood to old age. It shows the power of repetition, which Goebbels so well understood. We have heard "Early to bed and early to rise makes a man healthy, wealthy, and wise" so often that we believe it without question, although when you analyze it, it is obviously hokum. It is hokum in all three claims, particularly the part about making you wealthy. Who is it who gets to the office at eight on the dot—the shipping clerk or the Chairman of the Board? I drowsed in Smith Field, thinking how successful the inventor of that slogan would be if he were alive today, and what he could do for cigarettes, soap, hair tonic, and soda pop.

Around noon I flicked on the television, and who should be there, looking directly into my eyes, but Senator Fay Sumner Knott. Marge said, "Isn't that a charming suit? I saw one like that at Best's the other day, only it was a different shade."

"Hush," I said, "I can't hear what she's saying."

"Oh, switch it off," said Marge. "She's only talking politics in the Senate. She *is* photogenic, isn't she?"

Then I heard something about N.R.P., and I concentrated on listening, instead of watching. For months, very likely, Fay had been waiting to insert her stinger into the Administration. If she hadn't miscalculated her timing, I shuddered to consider the consequence. As it was, it was bad enough.

She was, obviously, just at the beginning of her speech in the Senate Chamber. The first thing I heard distinctly was that the N.R.P. was a total failure, and worse, a public scandal.

"I speak at a critical moment," she said. "News has just reached us that in Outer Mongolia there are two men capable of perpetuating the human race. Now I do not begrudge the Communists the right to continue, but think what it would mean if the world were swarming with Communistic Mongols?"

She smiled, and paused so that her listeners would have time for the picture to sink in. "Our most critical and vital resource," she went on, "is one man—Mr. Adam. And what has the Administration done about Mr. Adam?

"The Administration is apparently unaware of the fact that people are dying every day, and nobody is being born—at least here in the United States. We don't know how many are being born in Russia. Not only has the N.R.P. failed to promote the conception of a single baby—although it has been provided with unlimited funds—but it has as yet announced no definite plans for utilizing Mr. Adam."

Not only that, Fay continued, but the Administration had allowed Mr. Adam to consort with a number of women. She herself had seen Mr. Adam drinking with a notorious actress. She understood, "from the highest military authorities," that there was a woman living with Mr. Adam even now.

She said she very much regretted being forced to expose this scandalous state of affairs. She was not one to interfere in anyone's private life. However, this was a matter of transcendent importance to the nation, and it was particularly important to the nation's womanhood. Was the eternal hope of motherhood to be forever condemned by the soiled politicians who, for the time being, composed the Administration clique?

Marge said, "Stephen, isn't this awful!"

"No," I said. "I think it's wonderful. Wait until people find out that the woman with whom he is living is only his wife."

"That doesn't make any difference."

"Don't be silly."

N.R.P. was nothing more or less than a gigantic boondoggle, Fay told us, and a swindle. Mr. Adam was being allowed to run wild on the taxpayers' money. She began to go into details. She mentioned "a woman known as The Frame, whole real name is Kitty Ruppe, and whose screen name is Kathy Riddell."

"I think she's catty," Marge said. "She's just jealous. I'd never vote for her."

"In her state," I pointed out, "there are more men than women. Otherwise she'd never have been elected in the first place."

Fay began to talk about tete-à-tete in the Footlight Club. It occurred to me that Mr. Adam's movements had been pretty closely watched, and when I pieced this together with her reference to "high military authorities," I could smell Phelps-Smythe.

The television's eye shifted so that it encompassed the whole Senate Chamber. An announcer's voice said, "The Senate Chamber, which was almost empty when Senator Knott began to speak, has been rapidly filling." You could see that was true, and I recognized several members of the House standing in the background, a certain indication that this was the day's main attraction on Capitol Hill.

The announcer said that Senator Knott had yielded the floor to Senator Frogham, and immediately Frogham's face, jowls hanging down like a tired bloodhound, appeared on our screen. He started off by saying that he was shaken by his colleague's revelations, although hardly entirely surprised. "This is a terrible blow at our democratic and capitalistic system. What's going to happen to free enterprise and everything? How can we tell our school children they can grow up to be President when there aren't any school children?" He suggested that the Senate form a committee to investigate the N.R.P., with Senator Knott as chairman.

Senator Knott reappeared, and said it had been a mistake to take Mr. Adam out of the hands of the military in the first place, and that she was sure that there was sabotage, "probably inspired by a foreign power," within the N.R.P.

I shut her off and climbed out of Smith Field. "Where are you going?" Marge asked.

"We're going to Florida. I just resigned."

"Oh, no you didn't," Marge said. "You're not going to let a bunch of politicians chase you out of your job. Remember, there are a lot of people depending on you—Maria, and Thompson, and poor Mr. Adam. You can't just run away and leave Mr. Adam in this mess."

I put on my trousers. The telephone rang, Marge answered it, and said it was Mr. Gableman, for me. "Tell him I'm not in. Tell him I just had apoplexy."

"Stephen," Marge said sweetly into the telephone, "wants me to tell you that he's not in or he has just had apoplexy."

I took the telephone and said, "It's me, Smith. I quit."

"Oh, you heard about it," said Gableman. "Well, you can't quit now while we're under fire. That's the worst possible thing to do. That's what starts an organization disintegrating. Anyway, what's the dope? We've got to get out a press release, fast. Who's the woman staying with Adam?"

"His wife."

"His wife!" I could hear Gableman sigh. "Why, that's not bad! That's not bad at all. But what about this tomato, The Frame?"

"Purely platonic," I lied. "It just turns out that they're both interested in archeology."

"Even if that's true, which I doubt, we're not going to say anything about it," said Gableman. "We will just give out a simple, dignified statement that Mr. and Mrs. Adam are living together. That'll create sympathy, and it'll make Knott seem like a gossipy bitch. But what about The Frame?"

"You don't have to worry about her," I told him, "because her studio doesn't want her to get involved. They know it would be bad box office."

"Well, then, there's hardly anything to worry about at all. It will all blow over in a couple of days."

"I suppose so," I said.

"We'll ride this out, all right, but you'd better come on back right away."

Suddenly I thought of Mary Ellen, and Adam, and Jane Zitter, and I wondered what was going on in suite 5-F, and whether Mary Ellen had scalped Homer by now, and whether he had confessed, and what the Knott blast would do to his nerves. "Okay," I agreed. "I'll get out to La Guardia and catch the first plane."

Marge said, "Thank goodness, you aren't ducking your responsibilities."

"It's not that," I said. "I'm just curious."

Marge helped me fix my tie. "Darling," she said, "won't you try some of Tommy Thompson's tonic, or whatever it is? I do wish you would try something because I do want you to be the father of my children."

"Preposterous!" I told her. "There are probably a thousand varieties of snake oil being consumed all over the world, and none of them are going to do any good. Your only chance of becoming a mother is for Homer to be the papa, unless, of course, it is true about the two Mongolians, and the Russians agree to share them with us. And when you consider how many women there are in the world, I don't think your chances are very good. Honestly I don't."

"I am going to have a baby," Marge said. "I am, I am!"

CHAPTER 8

On the Washington plane I sat next to a man who said his name was Seymour Foreman, and that he was in real estate in Hartford. He asked me if I'd heard the news and I said I had. He said it was a terrible state of affairs, and that by God he was going to retire and spend the rest of his life fishing. He complained that now that he was able to get building materials in quantity, and architects could let their imagination run in designing new and smart low-cost homes, nobody wanted to build houses any more. "It is this way," he explained: "People don't build houses for themselves. They build for their children. And if they're not having any more children they're not having any more new homes. I don't see why Washington doesn't lash this Adam down and at least start token production."

I told him, logically I thought, that Adam was like an oil well. You had to be very patient and careful in bringing in the well, else the production might gush for only a short time, and then stop altogether. By practising conservation, the future of the race could be assured. This was particularly important when you considered that research was going forward to utilize all Mr. Adam's capabilities, instead of A.I. being forced to use the present wasteful methods.

That was all right, Foreman pointed out, but meanwhile the real estate and construction business was getting shaky. If he were in automobiles, or washing machines, or drug stores, or haberdasheries it would be different. Some businesses were not affected. But who wanted to invest in an apartment house when there was a good chance that two generations hence it would be inhabited solely by the rats, and a few surviving octogenarians? The trouble with real estate, there wasn't any future in it.

I said, "Mr. Foreman, that is the whole point. If we don't handle Mr. Adam properly, there will be anarchy."

"Well," he growled, "Washington had better get on the ball, or there won't be a businessman in the United States—big or little—who will support the Administration in the next elections."

"What difference will that make?" I inquired. "The Republicans are just as sterile as the Democrats. The only solution is to make A.I. work."

Mr. Foreman looked at me sharply, as if he had not really seen me before. "Do you work for the government?" he asked.

"Yes," I admitted. "Temporarily."

"Do you know anybody in the N.R.P.?"

"Uh-huh."

"Well, you better tell them the public is damned sick and tired of this fooling around. Now you take my daughter. She graduates from college this year, and majored in Home Economics. Boy, is she mad!"

In seventy minutes I learned a good many things I hadn't realized before about how things had gone since W.S. Day. For instance, practically nobody was getting married, but lots of people were living together. Manufacturers of baby shoes, in Massachusetts, had already closed down, and the toy business was acknowledged on the rocks. The Hays Office, in Hollywood, had banned all reference to motherhood, or babies, as being too painful a subject to portray on the screen. Fanny Brice, in the interests of good taste, abandoned her radio role of Baby Snooks. The school teachers had formed an association, looking towards the future, to concentrate on adult education. Harvard University was spending several millions to gather a compendium of all man's knowledge, and bury it in time capsules, in case A.I. failed, Darwin was right, and man would again evolve from some lower species. The undertakers seemed to have the only business with a future.

Eight-column banner headlines greeted me in Washington. They all said the same thing—"ADAM LIVING WITH WIFE!"—which showed that within a few hours the shrewd Gableman had managed to counteract Fay Knott's blast in the Senate. But apprehension harried me until I entered the Adam suite in the Shoreham.

When I rang the ball Jane opened the door a crack, and then released a chain latch. "What's the matter?" I asked.

"Reporters. Photographers. In regiments."

"Did you let them in?"

"Sure. I didn't want them to pound the place into splinters. No interviews, though. I told them any official statement would have to come from either you or Mr. Gableman. Just pictures."

"What kinds of pictures?"

"Chummy pictures. Pictures of Homer and Mary Ellen together."

"Doing what?"

"Oh, in the kitchen washing dishes—she washing and him drying; and Mary Ellen sitting on the side of a chair while he read; and playing gin rummy—all sort of homelike."

I kissed Jane on the nose. Jane's nose isn't quite sure what part of her face it ought to grace, but at that moment it seemed beautiful. There is nothing like a nice, chummy picture to drive the snakes of scandal out of the home. "You're a smart girl," I said, "and the Civil Service Commission shall hear about this, in an expurgated version, and the first thing you know you will have your classification raised."

"That's wonderful," Jane said.

"How's Mary Ellen taking it? What has she done to Adam?"

"It's amazing," Jane said. "It's positively amazing. She didn't do a thing to him. She just said she thought she understood, and that so far as she was concerned she knew it was strictly archeological, and he shouldn't worry about it. They're in the kitchen now, having a drink."

I went into the little kitchenette, one of those hotel affairs with a lot of glasses, very few plates, and hardly any silver. There they were, as Jane said, having a drink. But Homer was about as relaxed as a high tension wire, and he was holding his glass as if he were afraid it would jump out of his hand. Conversely, Mary Ellen appeared unworried and gay. She was wearing a starched, cotton something that was so perfect you wanted to surround her with cellophane and put her on the back cover of a magazine as the happy wife with vacuum cleaner.

"Hello, Steve," Homer said, keeping his eyes on the floor.

"Hello, Steve," said Mary Ellen. "I was just telling Homer he shouldn't worry. All big men have this sort of thing happen to them. Look at Lincoln. They maligned him, too. I do think Homer is Lincolnesque, don't you, Steve?"

"Sure," I said, "at least."

"He shouldn't let this thing worry him. It's all politics, isn't it Steve?"

"Oh, absolutely," I said. I kept wondering what was going on in her head, back of the wide-set gray eyes.

Homer lifted his head, started to speak, thought better of it, and gulped at his drink instead. I knew what Homer was thinking. He was a convulsive tangle of remorse, guilt, and downright fear. "Oh Lord," he managed finally, "I wish I was like other men."

"Other men," I said gallantly, "wish they were like you."

"I want to speak to Steve alone for a moment," Mary Ellen said. "You don't mind, Homer?"

"Oh, no, certainly not," Homer said, and he went out of the kitchenette faster than I had ever seen him move before.

Mary Ellen didn't speak immediately. She whirled the ice in her glass, lit a fresh cigarette, and then looked at me directly a few seconds with those level gray eyes. I recognized the look. I've had it from Marge a few times. It is grim business. "It was pretty lucky for the N.R.P. that I happened to be in Washington, here with Homer, when this thing blew up in the Senate today," she said. "Or did you plan it that way?"

"Who do you think I am, Machiavelli, Junior?"

"I wouldn't be surprised. I wouldn't be a bit surprised if you didn't encourage Homer to run around with that girl just to get his mind off the responsibilities of his home, so he'd go quietly when you were ready to lead him to the slaughter."

I had to know how much she knew. "Exactly what do you think went on between Homer and Kathy Riddell?" I asked.

"I think I can tell you exactly," Mary Ellen said calmly. "I think she seduced him—probably only once—after very careful preparation."

"Did Homer tell you that?"

"Certainly not! And if he started to tell me about it I wouldn't let him, because if he ever told me I'd have to give him up. And that I am not going to do!" I knew she meant it. "Poor Homer," she continued, "is transparent as that window pane. He's so honest, and decent, and gentle, and kind that when he tries to lie you just have to feel sorry for him. Why I knew—the first night I got here. He told me about this Kathy—and her archeology—and how nice it was to meet someone with mutual interests, and asked me whether I minded."

"You knew?"

"Certainly I knew. Women always know, although most times they won't even admit it to themselves, and they try to tell themselves that there is a chance they're mistaken, and they don't want to make any false accusations. They do that because their husband's infidelity presents a problem they're afraid of facing. They'd rather pretend it didn't happen. They're weak. I'm not."

"No," I agreed, "you're certainly not weak, Mary Ellen."

The straight line of her chin held firm, but her eyes suddenly misted. "You see, I love Homer. I'll always love him. That's why I can't afford to be weak, or delude myself, if I'm ever going to get him back. I'm just a plain woman, Steve. I'm no glamour-puss. I'm only going to have one man who really, honestly loves me, and that man is Homer. So by golly I'm going to fight for him."

"That's fine, and most laudable, and I'm in favor of it," I told her, "but look at the position—"

"You're going to tell me about humanity, and my duty to the country, but it doesn't affect me at all. I don't like the idea of Homer being used to fertilize ten million women, by the artificial insemination method, any better than I like the idea of him sleeping with The Frame."

"I think you're being narrow-minded. It is an entirely different matter. As a matter of fact, after our medical advisory committee eliminates waste from the methods of A.I., there isn't any reason why you and Homer shouldn't lead an entirely normal married life. The doctors will need him, perhaps, only a few days out of each month."

"I still don't like it," Mary Ellen said. "Have you ever considered my side of it?"

"Only in a general way," I admitted. "But now I begin to understand how you feel."

"At first I was just overwhelmed and terribly frightened," Mary Ellen explained. "I didn't dare argue about anything, or say a word about my rights. It was just too—colossal. Then when they took Homer away I couldn't think of anything to do. I'd cry all night, every night. If it hadn't been for Mrs. Brundidge—she made me get a grip on myself. Then I made all sorts of wild plans. I was going to kidnap Homer, or appeal to the Supreme Court. But I knew

I wouldn't get any sympathy, especially from the women. People would just say I was jealous, and selfish. Well, I am jealous, damn it!"

I wondered how much Mary Ellen was going to complicate the plans of N.R.P. "What do you propose to do?" I asked.

"I know that there isn't anything I can do at the moment about A.I.," Mary Ellen said. "All I want, now, is for Homer to stay in love with me. I'm more afraid of one woman than I am of millions."

"I think you're wise."

"You'll help me, won't you, Steve?"

"I certainly will," I agreed. "After all, I'm working for the government, and I have a job to do for the N.R.P., and I can't let them down. But from now on, you can depend on me to keep a tight rein on Homer. I'll admit I thought it was a good idea, at the time, for Homer to go out with The Frame. He has all sorts of inhibitions, as you probably know better than I do, and I thought if a good-looking girl gave him a lot of attention it would help break them down. I didn't have any idea it would go as far as it did."

"And I can stay here?"

"You can stay," I promised, "as long as the doctors agree it is okay."

It was a promise I couldn't make good. In a few days the storm caused by Fay Sumner Knott's charges concerning *l'affaire* Frame died down, but at once a new and disquieting murmur spread over the land.

It burst into public, of all places, on the prim editorial page of the Washington *Evening Star.* The *Star* began by saying it had always been in favor of the Home, and Marriage, just as it had always been against Evil, and Disease. But in view of the fact that it had received so many letters on the subject it felt obligated to present the views of what appeared to be a large portion of its readers.

The *Star* carefully backed into its editorial by recalling that during the war the government maintained a rigid control of strategic and critical materials. It recalled the stern measures taken to guard our precious supply of uranium at the time that the atomic bomb was being developed. Mr. Adam was a far more important substance than uranium, and there was obviously less of Mr. Adam than there was of uranium.

The *Star* then delicately inquired whether the government was doing its full duty to future generations when Mr. and Mrs. Adam lived under the same roof, and presumably occupied the same bed. Adam, the *Star* said, was a vital and limited national property, and in this case the rights of the nation, and indeed of the world, must be placed above Marriage and the Home.

The Washington *Times-Herald* said practically the same thing, but in a somewhat different way, on the following day, under a caption which read: "Is This Treason?"

The *Times-Herald* said that it didn't matter much whether Homer Adam was involved with The Frame, or whether he was involved with his wife. In either case, it was negligence on the part of the Administration. It was certainly sabotage, and possibly treason.

The *Times-Herald* significantly recalled the story of the two unspoiled Mongolians, which Moscow had never denied. Had Communist agents infiltrated into the upper brackets of N.R.P.? It certainly looked like it. And if they had, what better way was there for the Communists to conduct a war of extermination against the United States than to sabotage Mr. Adam?

The answer, of course, was very simple. Place Mr. Adam under the strictest military guardianship, and conduct a nice, short, preventive war against Russia before it was too late.

On the day following—a Thursday—all the newspapers bristled with letters-to-the-editor, mostly of female origin, protesting against Mrs. Adam, and the reporters on Capitol Hill said Congress was being swamped with mail.

Homer and Mary Ellen naturally were aware of what was going on, and they were both fretful and jumpy. On this Thursday I had driven them to Mount Vernon in an N.R.P. sedan, ostensibly so they could soak up some colonial atmosphere, but actually to keep them away from the radio. I tried talking about everything else except what was on their minds, but I could see it wasn't working. When we returned, Jane called from the office: "I've been trying to get you all day," she said. "Hell is popping. Everybody is taking turns stabbing you in the back, as if you were a human dart board. They all say you're responsible."

"I am," I said.

"They're after your job," Jane warned.

"They can have my job, and they can take it, and—"

I noticed that Mary Ellen was at my shoulder. "Mr. Pumphrey just sent you a memo—a red memo—" Jane continued. "He says it is imperative that you attend the meeting of the Planning Board at ten tomorrow."

"All right," I said. "I'll be there."

The Planning Board, on Friday morning, looked like the directors of a bank who have just been informed that the cashier has departed with all the liquid assets. When I entered, they regarded me as if I were the cashier. Gableman and Klutz shifted as far as possible from my chair, to avoid contamination. Pumphrey, his baggy face a mottled purple, stared at me as if I had just made an attack on his life. "I am very glad to see you here, Mr. Smith," he said. "I hardly need to tell you that this is a crisis!"

Sitting as observers, their chairs against the wall, and looking pious and complacent as good little boys watching a fight from the other side of the street, sat the liaison officers for the War, State, Interior, and Navy Departments, the Public Health Service, and the National Research Council. In a corner, inconspicuous as possible, sat Danny Williams, the President's Secretary, who used to be on the Washington Bureau of A.P. He was unsmiling and grave, but when I glanced at him, one owlish eye closed in a wink. They were all watching me. I didn't say anything.

"We all have had the greatest confidence in you," Pumphrey said. "But now we feel we have been betrayed. Do you hear that, Mr. Smith—betrayed!"

"I don't see what's so terrible in letting Homer Adam stay with his wife for a while," I said. "You asked me to get him into shape so that we could start A.I. That's what I've been doing. If any of you think you can handle Homer better, I'll be perfectly happy to step out. I'll be more than happy. I'll be delirious with joy."

Into the eyes of Percy Klutz came the wild gleam I had seen before. "It is exactly as I thought all along," said Klutz. "It is too big a task for one man. What we need is an entire new organization, and I have drawn up an entire new organizational chart."

Before anyone could stop him he sprang to his feet, and unrolled a six-foot chart from a map case on the wall. "Now," he said, "you will see that everything is almost the same, except up at the top, here, where we had Mr. Smith, and down here in Operations. We restore the committee, as originally planned, to direct policy on Mr. Adam. It will be a somewhat larger committee than first suggested, so it will include the State Department. Is that all right with you, Colonel Phelps-Smythe?"

Phelps-Smythe, who had been sitting with folded arms, his chair tilted back, enjoying himself, came erect, and said, "That's all right with the War Department. My general has instructed me to say that the War Department's chief concern is in security. Now I don't have to point out that if the War Department had been left in charge of Adam's field security, nothing like this would have happened."

"Oh, I've provided for that," said Klutz. "Right down here." He indicated a row of boxes at the bottom of the chart. "I'll get to that in a minute. First, we will take care of Mr. Smith. You don't mind, do you, Mr. Smith?"

"I don't mind."

"Well, Mr. Smith continues as Special Assistant to the Director, but his functions change somewhat. He becomes more of a liaison man between the policymaking committee and the operations end. You see, he will have a number of assistants who will take actual charge of Mr. Adam. There will be assistants in charge of security, housing, recreation, health, and so forth."

"That doesn't sound bad, Percy," said Abel Pumphrey.

"Just a matter of simple reorganization," said Percy proudly. "Every agency has them."

"Do you think it will quiet all this criticism?" Pumphrey asked. He looked at Gableman.

"I should think so," said Gableman, "provided Adam is separated from Mrs. Adam."

"What do you say, Mr. Smith?"

"I say it stinks," I said. "If you put Adam in a straitjacket again, he'll just get sick, or go nuts. Then where will you be?"

Danny Williams, who hadn't said anything thus far, spoke. "Instead of all this chart business," he asked, "wouldn't it be better if Adam just started having babies?"

"Naturally," said Abel Pumphrey, "that's ah, what we're all after. That's our motto—production, production, and more production."

"Well, Steve," Williams asked me, "do you think Adam is in good enough shape to start producing?"

"I think he's about ready," I replied, "but I wouldn't like to say for certain until the medical advisers okayed it."

"And if A.I. started, all this criticism would end, wouldn't it?" said Pumphrey.

"Oh, absolutely," said Gableman, "providing, as I said, his wife was out of the picture."

"That's what the President thought," said Williams. "The President thought that if Adam's health had improved we should just put him into production. I suppose that both from a political and a medical standpoint we had better separate Mr. and Mrs. Adam for the time being. But I don't think there's any need for all this reorganization."

That, of course, settled it. At least I thought it did. Klutz, dejected as an inventor who has been told his perpetual motion machine won't work, rolled up his chart. Phelps-Smythe looked sour and grumbled something I didn't quite catch, but which obviously concerned me. I said that if the doctors okayed it, production could begin Monday.

When I returned to Adam's suite Mary Ellen was packing. She was crying without any noise. Tears kept coming into her eyes, and she'd wipe them with the back of her hand, but she wasn't letting even a sniffle escape her. Finally she turned to me and said, "You don't have to tell me to get out. I knew when you got that call last night that I'd have to go."

"Now take it easy, Mary Ellen," I told her. "It could be a lot worse."

"What did they decide?" she asked.

"Well, they decided that A.I. had to start right away. That was the first thing. And they thought it best that you and Homer separate for a while. Anyway, it would be pretty embarrassing for you to stay just at this time, now wouldn't it, Mary Ellen?"

"I don't think so," she said in a small voice. "I don't think it would be so terribly embarrassing."

"Oh, sure it would," I told her, trying to sound convincing. "Anyway, this separation is just temporary. Just as soon as production levels off, and is placed on a sound basis, you and Homer will be able to be together again."

"I wish I thought so."

"What makes you think it won't happen?"

She stood up, very straight, unashamed of her tears and her anger. "It's that girl—The Frame. She's after him again!"

"After him?"

"She called him from California this morning. What does she want? Why does she keep after him?"

"What do any of them want? She wants to have a baby, I guess."

"No, it's deeper than that. Steve, I'm afraid. I'm terribly afraid!"

I remembered the glimpse of the fanatic The Frame's face had unmasked just before she boarded her plane. In a vague sort of way, I was afraid, too, but all I said was, "Stop worrying. I'll take care of anything that comes up. Did you say anything to Homer?"

"No. I was with him in the living room when the call came in, and afterwards I asked who it was, and he told me, and all I could say, naturally, was how nice that she had called."

"What did he tell her?"

"He just grunted, and said yes and no. Of course he knew I was listening."

"Where's Homer now?"

"In the kitchen, brooding."

I went into the kitchenette. Homer was staring into a tumbler of milk as if he expected something to poke its head out of it. I told him about the meeting of the Planning Board. It didn't seem to affect him any more than if I were describing a Friday afternoon session of the Hyannis, Nebraska, PTA. I said, "I understand Kathy called this morning."

"Yes," and then: "Steve, I can't forget her. I keep thinking about her all the time."

"Mary Ellen," I told him, "loves you. Mary Ellen is taking a terrific beating, without complaining. Mary Ellen is my nomination as a swell wife."

"Oh, I know it, Steve. Mary Ellen is wonderful. But how can I help it if I keep thinking of Kathy? I can't control my thoughts, can I?"

"I suppose not," I said. I told him he'd get his final physical the next day, and that A.I. would begin on Monday, if everything went according to schedule. He didn't seem to mind. He kept staring at things without seeing them, and I wondered what The Frame had told him that made him act like he was the central figure in a hashish dream.

We took Mary Ellen to the station and put her on the New York train. They seemed to have a lot of things to say to each other, but they didn't mean anything. She would write every day, and tell him how Eleanor was getting along. He would write every day, too. She hoped he wouldn't have to be away from the baby so long—he should see how she was changing. He said he was sure Steve would fix it up for him to visit Tarrytown, but not just now of course. She said she didn't think this A.I. would be as bad as he expected. He said he supposed he would get used to it.

I told Mary Ellen that pretty soon she should buy some spring clothes, and send me the bill, because all that was included in the N.R.P. budget, and she should buy all she wanted.

She leaned down from the train steps and kissed him. She kissed him hard, and clung to him. I knew what she was thinking. She was thinking that probably she would not see him again.

Back in the hotel, I telephoned Tommy Thompson, and he promised to be in Washington in the morning. "I'll bring a surprise for you," he said.

Homer and I played gin until midnight. The twelve o'clock news led off with an excited announcement that, doctors willing, A.I. would begin on Monday. As yet, the identity of the first A.I. mother, "destined to again carry forward the banners of humanity," had not been revealed.

CHAPTER 9

Dr. Thompson arrived in the morning. He didn't come alone. He brought Marge, Maria Ostenheimer, and J.C. Pogey. "This is the visiting delegation," he explained. "I hope you have room for us."

I told him to look around, and pick their own bedrooms. We had them to spare. "All except you," I told Marge. "You know where you sleep."

"Yes, darling," Marge said, docilely.

"Why are you being so nice to me? What are you up to?"

"Why, nothing, sweetheart. Aren't you glad to see me?"

"Certainly I'm glad to see you, but when you get sugary like this I know that you're up to something, or you've done something bad."

Maria said that was nonsense, and that, as she always knew, I was a nasty and suspicious man. J.C. Pogey went prowling around, and said that the Adam suite was a classic example of government waste. He had counted eight bedrooms, and six baths, and there were only three people living in it, if you included Jane, who sometimes spent the night.

"I'll tell you how it is," I explained. "If A.I. doesn't work, we're going to use it as a sort of high-class male brothel." Marge said I ought to be ashamed, and that I had shocked Homer, and indeed this was true, for his face was the color of his hair.

I noticed that Tommy kept watching Homer, closely, not saying anything. But I wasn't worried, because Homer appeared to be in good spirits, his seizures of the shakes seemed to have deserted him, and he was even talkative.

At eleven o'clock Tommy and I took Homer to the U.S. Public Health Service for his examination. There were nine or ten doctors, representing all the departments and agencies that had their hand on the erratic pulse of this important human. They inspected him for an hour, and then went into conference for a few minutes, and then they came out and Tommy told me, "He's okay. We're getting out an official report—that is, the Surgeon General will get it out—but the main thing is that you can use Homer Adam on a limited scale."

"What do you mean, 'limited scale'?" I asked.

"Well, so long as everything goes along evenly, we can use Adam for the impregnation of, say, two or three women a week. After he gains more weight and his metabolism perks up he can be used more frequently, providing that there are no glandular disturbances. Of course, if he were subjected to great emotional shock, or his general physical condition started to get worse instead of better, then we'd have to call it off. But for now, you can go ahead."

I almost shouted. I'm afraid I ran to the telephone like a cub reporter with his first flash. I called Abel Pumphrey, and gave him the news, and then I called Danny Williams at the White House. Danny was a little cagey, and made me repeat everything Tommy had said, and then he asked me: "I suppose you feel your job's over now?"

I said, "I have only one life to give for my country, and believe me, bud, I have given it!"

"Oh, no you haven't," he told me. "We'll be satisfied when A.I. is S.O.P.*"

"That's not fair, Danny," I pleaded. "I only agreed to get Adam in condition for production. I've got my own life to lead."

"I could give you a lecture," Danny said, "on national responsibility. But I do not think it is necessary. You know damn good and well that your job hasn't ended. What about your wife? Do you want her to be childless? For that matter, do you want to be childless? Do you want to pass out of this world without perpetuating the name of—" he hesitated—"Stephen Decatur Smith, the second."

"Okay, Danny," I surrendered. "But when things are S.O.P., I'm finished."

"When it is all over," Danny said, "the President will no doubt give you an award of the Legion of Merit."

I remembered Colonel Phelps-Smythe. I started out to tell Danny what he could do with the Legion of Merit, pointed end first, but at that moment Tommy touched me on the shoulder, and said the car was there, and he and Homer were waiting.

So we went back to the party. Perhaps I had better explain. It wasn't a party when we left, but it was a party when we got back. You cannot put a lot of people in a large number of rooms with an unlimited assortment of free liquor, and an excuse, and not have a party. The excuse was the beginning of A.I., and they had anticipated the verdict before we returned. As a matter of fact, when I look back on it, any other verdict seemed impossible. On that day, even if Homer Adam were drawing his last breath, gasping like a fish long out of water, still he would have been approved for A.I. I guess we were all pretty desperate.

Everybody treated Homer as if he had just made a winning touchdown, and he seemed to like it. You cannot exactly say that he stuck out his chest, but at least his habitual slump straightened,

---

* Artificial insemination is standard operating procedure.

in the manner of all men who have been thumped and probed by the doctors, and told they will live. But he stayed around the telephone. Whenever our phone rang, Homer answered. Long before I'd arranged to have all our calls screened. That is, I'd left a selected list of people who could call and get straight through. Other calls were referred to N.R.P. Finally Homer answered the telephone and didn't call me, or Jane, or J.C. Pogey, or anyone else to it. He simply seemed to curl around it. I edged toward him, but I didn't hear much. Just yes, and no, and grunts.

When he had finished, I went downstairs to the switchboard. "There was just a call for Mr. Adam," I said. "Where did it come from?"

"Oh, that one. From L.A."

"Who authorized calls from L.A. up into 5-F?"

"Why, Mr. Smith," the girl said, surprised. "Mr. Adam himself did! We don't screen any calls from Miss Kathy Riddell."

"How long has that been going on?"

"Why, ever since Miss Riddell was in Washington."

I said "thank you," and went back upstairs. There wasn't much, or anything, that I could do about it. I didn't want to start anything that would send Homer off on some unpredictable tangent. I simply wanted to maintain the status quo. Anyway, in a few days it wouldn't matter, I thought. Homer would be so busy re-populating the earth that not even The Frame would interest him.

I don't think J.C. Pogey was a good influence on Homer. That afternoon we were all sitting around, and Marge was acting as bartender, and Tommy Thompson was telling us about his experiments which he hoped would revive the male germ through medicine. It seems his first batch of seaweed lotion, or whatever it was, hadn't been successful. Some fellows got sick, but no wives got pregnant. So he had revised the formula.

"Wouldn't it be grand if it worked," Homer said. "Imagine, I could— why I could do whatever I wanted. I'd be just like everybody else!"

"I don't see anything good about it," said J.C., "any more than I see any real sense in torturing Homer Adam, here, simply because he was the victim of an oversight. You—" he pointed a lean finger at Tommy—"exhaust yourself trying to combat destiny. Why don't you take that girl—" he shifted his finger towards Maria—"out into the woods somewhere and forget all about the so-called human race. This little globe we live on has grown old, as I have, and God has simply decided to eliminate it. When Mississippi blew up God could just as easily have allowed the world to blossom as a nova. Instead, he is going to let it die like the last coal in the grate. Why fight it?"

Maria had been sitting on the arm of Tommy's chair, one small hand on his massive shoulder. She waited for Tommy to speak, and when he did not, she said, quietly, "I think I can tell you why Tommy works, and why I work, Mr. Pogey. We are fighting for more than our lives. We are fighting to keep intact the thread that ties us to the hereafter. Man's only link with immortality is through his children. That's why we want the world to keep on having babies."

J.C. Pogey shook his head in unhappy denial. "You're taking the short view," he said. "I take the long view. This particular sphere is only one of unnumbered millions stretching out across uncountable light years. Some of these spheres probably carry creatures which also fancy they have souls, and that they are linked with the Almighty. We would be very self-centered to think otherwise."

"I'll agree," Maria argued, "that there must be some kind of life on other planets, perhaps in other constellations, but you can't call it human."

"Depends on what you term human," said J.C. Pogey. "Now I can imagine a human being on some other globe. He might have four heads and eight arms. If we saw him we'd consider him a monstrosity, simply because he would be a bit unusual. But think how much better off he would be than we humans who have only one head and two arms. One brain might be a whiz at mathematics and a second at literature and another at philosophy and the fourth might just like to raise hell. Think of the fun he'd have."

Marge said she thought J.C. was crazy, and that furthermore he made her feel frightened, but Homer was listening, fascinated. "If that's true," he said, "it wouldn't be so bad if I—failed, would it?"

"Not at all," J.C. said.

"Don't listen to him, Homer," Marge said. "He's just a nasty sacrilegious old man."

"On the contrary," said J.C., "the only thing that makes me retain my sanity, and my belief in the Deity, is that this is a third-class world which God doesn't take very seriously. It is like a rotten fruit that has hung too long upon the tree. God has simply become bored with running this world, and is closing it down."

"Then you don't think A.I. will work?" Homer asked, with the utter faith of a woman asking a question of a swami.

"Frankly, no," J.C. replied. "I think you are just an accident, Homer, an oversight that will be remedied. You shouldn't have been down in that shaft when Mississippi blew up."

I could see that Homer was impressed. "Now look, J.C.," I said. "Stop putting those silly ideas into Homer's head. Just because you're too old to have children yourself, you shouldn't discourage everybody else in the world."

J.C. snorted. "I don't believe it," he said. "Fate's against it."

"A.I. starts Monday," I said. "On Monday everything begins again."

A few hours later I began to think J.C. Pogey was right. Gableman and Klutz came to see us. I thought they were coming in to join the celebration, but they seemed distraught and worried. "Bring Mr. Gableman and Mr. Klutz a drink," I told Marge. "And honey, change the brand. Every drink I've had this afternoon tastes funny."

"Has it, dear?" Marge asked. "I'm sorry. Perhaps I'm mixing them wrong. I'll do better."

Gableman signaled me with a nod, and we went into a huddle in a corner. "Hell to pay," he said. "The office is a madhouse."

"What's wrong?"

Klutz said, "Well, this thing took us rather suddenly—I mean putting Adam into production right away—and quite truthfully, we don't seem to be prepared for it."

"I don't see why not," I told him. "Everything is simple enough now. Homer is okay. I'll just take him down to the lab Monday morning, and by Monday night some worthy female will be pregnant."

"That's just it," Klutz said. "How do we pick the worthy female?"

"You don't mean to tell me," I said, "that with practically every woman in the United States wanting to become a mother—even women who never wanted to be mothers before—that you have trouble picking one!"

Klutz drew a pencil from his pocket, and paper. He seemed incapable of thought or speech unless they were accompanied by doodles. "It is far more complicated than that!" he said. "It is complicated beyond anything anyone imagined! It is a major matter of policy that should have been decided, long ago, by the Inter-Departmental Committee, on the highest level, mind you. For whomever we pick as the first A.I. mother, all the other women will raise a howl, and it is bound to have political repercussions!"

"That sounds insane," I commented. I looked up, and saw Homer's gaunt form behind me, swaying slightly. He was listening, and he did not seem amused.

"Oh, no," said Gableman. "It is not insane at all. Consider the factors involved. In the first place—and this is really minor—there is the matter of geography. Every state wants priority on production, and the honor of furnishing the first A.I. mother."

"That shouldn't be hard," I pointed out. "After all, while Homer's capacity is to be limited for the time being, each section of the country can be represented in the first group of mothers selected."

Gableman ran his long, unwashed hands through his long, oily hair. "As I said," he persisted, "that is the simplest part. Then you get into race, religion, and social and economic position. The Negro question is particularly vexing. Do you know what the Southern Democrats in the Senate are doing? They're planning to legislate N.R.P. out of existence unless we follow an All White policy. And the Negro press is screaming that we will be murdering the race unless we follow at least a policy of fifty-fifty.

"And take religion. There are some people who think that this is a fine opportunity to eliminate the Catholics, or the Jews, and naturally the Catholics and Jews are afraid of just this and they are demanding guarantees against extinction."

I noticed that J.C. Pogey and Marge had joined our little group. Pogey's face showed no emotion, but I knew he was laughing inside himself. "I think it is ridiculous," I said. "The thing to do is get it started. Why, look at Marge here. She's an average woman, and most of all she wants things to begin again, don't you dear?"

"I wouldn't mind having an Adam child, if that's what you mean," Marge said, smiling at Homer. "As a matter of fact, I'd like one very much."

"Now that wouldn't do at all, if I may say so," Gableman said seriously. "Then people would charge the Administration with a sort of new-fangled nepotism."

Klutz's pencil continued to work. "And that isn't by any means all," he went on. "That is just the beginning. Suppose we pick a nice, average, Presbyterian, white, not rich not poor housewife, of good character. Well, all the unmarried women will say she's already had her chance, and didn't do anything about it, and that they, the un-married women who never had a chance should have one now. Then, of course, the veterans' wives have been asking for priority—and cer-tainly this should be considered, with elections coming up next year—but so have the Wacs and the Waves. Who should have the priority, the wives or the service-women? Dear, dear, I should think that this is the most perplexing problem that N.R.P. has ever faced." Klutz stared at us. Obviously, it was so monumental he could say no more.

Gableman took it up. "When the State Department heard that A.I. was authorized to begin Monday, it immediately protested to the President, because it had not been kept fully informed. The State Department is conducting the most delicate negotiations on how to share Adam. It is so delicate because of the two Mongolians."

"May I say something?" Homer asked timidly.

Gableman didn't hear him. "You see, the international situation is this way. The State Department doesn't want to be accused of appeasing Russia, but if there actually are two Mongolians then we want to be big-hearted, and offer Russia a good slice of Adam. However, nobody knows whether there are two Mongolians or not, and until the State Department finds out, they do not want to be committed to a program. They have given us an order to do nothing hasty."

"Pardon me a moment," Homer interrupted. "I was just going to say—"

"Yes," Klutz said. "I am afraid we have been caught flat-footed. I think we should have a group of experts draw up recommendations to present to the Planning Board, which in turn will work out a proposal which will be presented to the Inter-Departmental Commitee, which then can draw up a directive for the approval of the President."

"Wait a moment!" Homer shouted. It was the first time I, or I suppose anyone else, had ever heard Homer Adam shout. It shocked us all into silence. Even Homer himself could not speak for a few seconds. But observing the surprising effect upon us all, apparently gave him courage, because he thrust out his chin as far as it would go and demanded: "Did it ever occur to you people that I might want to have something to say about this matter? It's me that's doing it, you know!"

Nobody said anything. "Why can't I pick my own brides?" Homer demanded.

"Oh, but you cannot really call them brides," Klutz protested. "It is doubtful whether you'll ever see any of them at all."

"The children," Homer said, "are going to be my children, and I think I should have something to say about what the mothers look like."

"Perhaps," Gableman suggested smoothly, "Mr. Adam is thinking of one certain person?"

"And what if I am?" said Homer. He looked angry enough to fight. "You stand up there and talk about splitting me up and dealing me out as if I were a tax rebate. Perhaps, so long as I am to be given away, I can give away a little of myself."

Marge shoved herself in front of me. "I think Homer is absolutely right," she said. "I think for the first one he should choose whoever he wants."

"You keep out of this!" I ordered her. "This is official business, and anyway I think you've got your mind set on being unfaithful to me."

Klutz held up his hands. "Now, Mr. Adam," he pleaded, "please be reasonable. The N.R.P.—and I am sure I am speaking for Mr. Pumphrey and the Planning Board—could not possibly allow you to allocate yourself. We would be accused of permitting you to set yourself up as a dictator—which indeed you would be. Why, if you picked the mothers, there wouldn't be much use of the N.R.P. continuing at all, would there? It would be contrary to the national interest."

Gableman rubbed his face, and his lower jaw worked as if in rhythm with deep thought. "Gentlemen, I think I can offer a solution," he said. "Why not pick the first A.I. mothers by lot, just the way soldiers are picked by the draft?"

"That sounds like a very sound idea," Klutz agreed. "The only thing is we'd have to register all the women who wanted to be mothers, which would consume much time. And in addition, if every single prospect for motherhood was allowed to register, the first choice might be one who would be extremely controversial, and then where would we be? I'm not sure N.R.P. could survive an unlucky choice."

"Well, let's put it in the lap of Congress," Gableman said. "We'll have each Senator and Congressman nominate two women—just like they nominate candidates for West Point—and then we'll give them numbers, and the President can pick a number out of that goldfish bowl we always use for those things."

"Say, that's fine," Klutz agreed. "I think that does it. But what about the international drawings, if we have any?"

"Oh, we'll leave that to the UN," said Gableman, "although the State Department won't like it."

"Well, thank goodness that's settled," said Klutz.

Homer, silent and white-faced, walked out of the room, down the hall, into his own bedroom, and shut the door. I didn't feel good about the way we'd treated Homer, but obviously, for his own best interests, I felt he should not be allowed to participate in this phase of things.

Later that evening a Special Agent from the FBI came to 5-F. He brought, as a safe hand messenger, the dossier of The Frame which I'd requested the day she left for the Coast. You'd think newspapermen would quit being surprised. They discover that kindly old gentlemen rape, and sometimes chop up, little girls; and church deacons garnish their wives' soup with arsenic over a period of years; and the impoverished old lady who has been on relief has three hundred thousand in cash stuffed in her mattress; and the lieutenant general who is a hero at home is a heel at the front. Newspapermen ought to quit being surprised, but they never do, and I was surprised at the dossier on The Frame. I had no more read the book of her life correctly than the man browsing through the library, who picks up a volume and reads an occasional sentence and paragraph here and there—skipping whole chapters—and lays it down in ten minutes.

I didn't even know how long she had lived. I thought The Frame was 25 or 26. She was 31. I didn't know she had been an honor student at her high school in Chicago, and later at the University of Chicago, although of course I knew her father was Professor Ruppe, the archeologist and scientist. She had taken her B.S. at Chicago, and then come to New York and danced.

In New York, too, she had a weird sort of double life, for even while she danced at that seedy uptown tourist trap she was taking a master's degree at Columbia.

In 1940 she had gone to Hollywood. She had become engaged to Dr. Alfred Magruder, the atomic physicist from Berkeley. He had been killed in the Mississippi explosion.

For two of the war years The Frame had been employed, along with her fiancé and her father, on the Manhattan Project. After the war she returned to Hollywood, making occasional visits to Bohr-ville.

She was the author of a number of brilliant papers on nuclear fission. On the Manhattan Project she had served as secretary and assistant to the renowned Dr. Felix Pell. The dossier ended: "Loyalty and patriotism unquestioned."

So that was The Frame! She seemed a most improbable person, and yet I knew the FBI would not be mistaken in any detail. Long after everyone else in the Adam suite had retired, I sat in the living room, staring into the shadowy vastness of Rock Creek Park, and trying to fit The Frame into the puzzle of Homer Adam. No matter how I arranged the pieces, she didn't seem to fit—except in one way, and that way so sinister that I instantly wanted to throw it out of my mind, just as the mind rejects and quickly forgets a dream too horrible to remember.

Yet it kept coming back—the possibility that The Frame's interest in Homer Adam was essentially directed at doing away with him, and in this way completing the death of mankind. I kept telling myself that, all in all, The Frame wasn't a bad sort of a girl, and the phrase in the FBI report, "loyalty and patriotism unquestioned," I revolved over and over, and yet the thought kept coming back to me.

It was altogether improbable. And yet was it any more improbable than Mississippi blowing up and wrecking me by an unseen, unfelt radiation without my even knowing it? Was it any more improbable than dropping a bit of material the size of an egg on a great city, and thereby reducing some hundreds of thousands of human beings to a few pinches of ashes?

It was not reasonable for The Frame to plot such a thing. And yet it is not reasonable for grown, mature men who go to church on Sundays, and are kind to their families, to spend the better part of their lives seriously plotting, in General Staff conferences, how to eliminate another nation, and most of its people, in the fewest number of days and hours.

I kept looking for a motive. She might be crazy, of course. She was probably a genius, and most of us believe that genius is a little crazy. Or perhaps, having lost her chance of happiness, she wished all others reduced to her level. This is a very peculiar, and often unnoticed, instinct of people. We saw it one day, in March, 1933, when the nation's economic inequalities were suddenly leveled by the bank holiday. Since for a time nobody had anything, and all were alike in poverty, everyone was relieved and happy.

I felt that I had to know more about The Frame's relations with Homer Adam, and right away. I went into his room. He had his face almost buried in the pillow, his long arms stretched around the crumpled pillow as if he had been crushing it. His feet extended, toes down, over the edge of the bed. He was asleep, and I shook him awake. "Hey?" he said. "What's the trouble?"

"Wake up, Homer, I want to talk to you."

"All right, Steve. Go ahead. Talk."

"You're not mad at me, are you?"

"No. Why?"

"I thought you would be sore because I didn't stick up for you when you said you wanted to pick the first A.I. mother."

"Oh, no, I'm not sore. I was just trying to do someone a favor."

"I suppose you wanted to pick Kathy for the first A.I. mother. In a way, I don't blame you. But I couldn't conscientiously encourage your request. It would cause a great stir, and it wouldn't be fair to Mary Ellen."

Homer turned over and sat up, his hair wild. He blinked the remnants of sleep out of his eyes and said, "Oh, no. I wasn't thinking of Kathy. I wasn't thinking of Kathy at all."

"Well, who were you thinking about?"

Homer seemed uncomfortable as if the bed were infested with red ants. "I'd rather not say."

"Oh, come on, Homer, you can tell me!"

"No, I don't think I'd better."

"Why, that's silly, Homer. If you are really set on picking some particular person, maybe I can fix it up. Perhaps it's Mary Ellen. Perhaps you'd like to have another child yourself. Nobody could blame you for that."

Homer didn't look at me. He looked at his hands, and he looked at the door, and he looked everywhere but at me. "No, it was not Mary Ellen," he said. He hesitated, and then blurted out, "If you have to know, Steve, it was Marge."

"Marge!" I tried to pull myself together. I knew that I should be urbane about it, and perhaps nonchalant, and that by no means should I alarm Homer, but I knew I wasn't succeeding.

"Please, Steve," Homer pleaded. "Please don't be angry. I was only trying to repay all your favors and your kindness. And I know that more than anything else Marge wants to have children, and she's always been so nice to me, and she said that she would be delighted to have an Adam child. She's hinted herself, several times today. She's always said she'd be proud to have one."

"Oh, she has, has she?"

"Yes. You see, Steve, that's all I have to give."

Well, I thought, I have to be broad-minded, and Homer is really being very decent and sincere, and there isn't any reason to be jealous. "That is really very decent and generous of you, Homer," I said. "I am touched. But I think that on behalf of the Smith family I must decline. As a matter of fact, as Gableman pointed out, people would call it nepotism, and charge graft and favoritism within the Administration. Why, it would be just like an official of the Department of the Interior deeding himself oil land owned by the government."

"Yes, I suppose so," said Homer. "But it seems to me that every time I want to do anything, myself, somebody blocks me. I ought to have some rights."

"Homer," I advised him, "I think you had just better dedicate yourself to unselfish service. You will be happier." I remembered my original mission in waking him. "Homer," I asked, "does Kathy want to have children?"

"No. I'm quite sure she doesn't."

"How sure?"

"Oh, I am absolutely sure. Absolutely. She said she wasn't ready to have children yet."

That answer fitted in with the theory I could not ignore. "Did Kathy ever suggest that you shouldn't go through with A.I.?"

Homer considered a few moments before he spoke, his bony fingers picking at the mauve blanket. "Not exactly," he said. "She said I was being used improperly, and she doesn't have a very high regard for the N.R.P."

"Did Kathy ever talk to you about nuclear fission, or anything like that?"

"Oh, no! All we've ever talked about was archeology—and us. If you don't mind Steve, I'd rather not go into it any further. You know how it is—it's very personal with me. I think at least that part of my life is private property."

"I can't help but agree with you," I told him. His answers left me not far from where I was in the beginning. Forget it, I said to myself. Forget it. If The Frame wanted to destroy Homer, she'd had plenty of opportunity that night in the hotel. I promised myself I would forget it, and that, as Maria always insisted, I had a naturally suspicious mind, and yet I knew I would not forget.

"Honestly," Homer said. "You're not sore about my suggesting—about Marge?"

"Not a bit, Homer. Go on to sleep. Just dismiss it from your mind."

"Thanks, Steve," he said, and fell back on the pillow.

I went to my bedroom and turned on the light and Marge instantly raised her head and said, "Stephen, this is a fine time to be getting to bed. It is—" she looked at her watch—"nearly three o'clock. If that's all you think of me you can just get into your own bed."

"Don't worry," I told her. "I will!"

"Stephen, what on earth is the matter with you?"

"There are a number of kinds of infidelity," I said, taking off my shoes and slamming them on the floor. "It isn't necessary to be physically unfaithful. You can be unfaithful in spirit. One is as bad as the other."

"Stephen, stop talking in riddles."

"You know what I'm talking about."

She made a face at me. "All right, then, stay over there in your own bed."

"You certainly have changed a lot," I said, "since this morning. This morning you were silky sweet to me. Now, you don't want me to touch you."

"I didn't say I didn't want you to touch me."

"Yes you did. You told me to get into my own bed."

She sat up, looking very pink and round and powdered and clean and smooth. "Stephen, you don't know a damn thing about women!"

I turned out the light.

CHAPTER 10

It was one of those awakenings when you know something is wrong, and for a while you cannot figure out what it is, and then you discover that it is yourself. My head felt floaty, as if it were filled with helium and wanted to disengage itself from my trunk, and my elbows and knees ached. When I sat up I definitely had white flashes and spots in front of my eyes. "Oh," I groaned. "I feel awful."

"That's too bad," said Marge, looking at me with deep interest. "What's the matter, hangover?"

"I didn't drink enough to have a hangover."

"Oh, I think you did," Marge said.

"No I didn't. I think I'm sick."

"Oh, I hope not," Marge said apprehensively. "I certainly hope not. I'll bring you some aspirin, and coffee."

The coffee tasted horrible. "You put salt in here," I accused her, "instead of sugar."

"No I didn't. Really I didn't, Stephen. Just stay in bed and you'll feel better. I'm sure you'll feel better."

"Call Tommy Thompson," I said. "I think I've got pneumonia, or something."

She got Thompson in a hurry. He was sleepy-eyed, and wearing a maroon dressing gown I suspect he had filched from the Army. He held my wrist, and felt my forehead, and looked under my eyelids. "Pulse is a little rapid," he said. "I don't see anything else wrong."

"When I look at things," I said, "they won't stand still. Things keep jumping around."

"Nerves," Thompson said. "Just plain nerves. You'll feel better in a little while. You ought to relax for a few days. Why don't you and Marge fly down to Florida?"

"Oh, no," I said. "We're in the last lap, now. I'm not going to leave here and have something happen. I want to get this job wrapped up, and finished. Then we'll take a vacation, won't we, dear?"

"It would be lovely," Marge said.

After thirty or forty minutes I began to feel better, as Thompson had predicted. But all day long everything I ate and drank tasted salty.

Tommy and Maria and J.C. Pogey went back to New York on the Congressional that afternoon, and Homer and Marge and Jane went to the station to see them off. The last thing Pogey said, he said to Homer. "Son," he told him, "if everything doesn't work out the way it is planned, don't feel too badly about it. Not your fault. It just wasn't set up to be that way." I never saw such an incorrigible pessimist.

Monday, on which we had hoped to begin A.I., passed, and the other days of the week trooped past after it. Generally, people seemed satisfied with the N.R.P. plan for selecting the first A.I. mother, and those who would be next in line. But Moscow wasn't satisfied, and said so very plainly. The Russians didn't mind selecting an American for the first A.I. mother, but the second ought to be Russian, and the third perhaps might go to Great Britain. As to the smaller states, they weren't to be considered until much, much later. As a matter of fact, the Russians didn't see any need for including Poles, Rumanians, Hungarians, Turks, Egyptians, or Persians in the plan at all. Those lands, the Russians said, could be re-populated any time, and the Soviet Union would be glad to attend to it. The State Department countered by asking Russia, for the tenth time, whether it was true about the two Mongolians. The Russians said this was strictly an internal matter.

Domestically, things were better. The Congress viewed the plan as an unexpected and welcome gift of patronage. Whenever a Congressman has a chance to give away something that doesn't belong to him, it is so much gravy. It was a splendid opportunity to pay off political debts, win social favor, and endear themselves with women's organizations. It was just ticklish enough, politically, to be exciting. And since the N.R.P. had placed a week's deadline on the nominations, they could always plead that the Administration forced them to choose in haste, in case their nominations failed to meet public approval. Some made their choices public—when they were absolutely certain they were politically foolproof. But most said they wouldn't divulge the names until the drawings.

In that week we took Homer down to the Eastern Shore, for fishing, and to Bowie for the opening of the spring racing season, and to the National Theater, and for a trip through the Shenandoah Valley, and by the time the next Monday rolled around Homer really appeared fairly healthy. I do not mean that he could go out and chop down trees. I merely mean that he looked as if he could beget a number of babies.

On noon Monday we went to the Capitol. That is, Marge and I went to the Capitol. We left Homer at the hotel, at his own insistence. He was fearful, and I suppose rightly, that he would receive an ovation if he were discovered sitting in a gallery while the drawing took place, and he was deathly afraid of public attention.

The drawing was held on the floor of the House, and the scene was so familiar, with its warlike connotation, that it seemed like looking at an old newsreel. Only this time it wasn't Wilson or Roosevelt wearing the blindfold.

When the preliminaries were over, the President reached his hand into the goldfish bowl and drew out a capsule and handed it to the Clerk of the House. He opened it, unfolded a slip of paper, and shouted into the banked microphones: "Number 646. The number is 646!"

Up from the well of the House there floated an excited feminine scream. "What was that?" Marge asked.

"Just an overwrought female," I said.

"I don't know," said Marge. "Do you know what it sounded like to me. It sounded just like when a woman wins a door prize at a bridge party, or right after she yells 'Bingo.' I wonder who had number 646?"

I noticed an unusual commotion in the Press Gallery. Ordinarily the Press Gallery moves swiftly and efficiently to get out the flash, but now it seemed to be erupting in all directions. "I'll find out what happened," I told Marge, left my seat, and worked my way down the corridor.

I ran into Bingham, the UP man. "How about a statement?" he asked before I had a chance to speak.

"On what?"

"Don't you know who he picked?"

"No."

"Number 646," Bingham said, "is held by Fay Knott."

"You mean one of her candidates?"

"No, by her, personally."

"I'm sorry," I said. "I feel sick. You'll have to excuse me." I did feel sick. The baroque tiled walls of the corridor were all leaning in towards me. I blundered my way back to Marge. "Let's go," I told her, "646 is Fay Sumner Knott. What a catastrophe! What a disaster!" I thought of the President. "That poor unlucky man," I said. "That poor, poor unlucky man!"

When we reached our car Marge asked, "But why did she nominate herself? I don't think that is fair."

"I suppose," I said, "Fay Sumner Knott couldn't find any other woman in her own state as admirable as herself. That's the way she figures, you know."

"What's going to happen?" Marge asked. "Can't you get it cancelled, or something? Is it really so bad?"

"Wait until I break the news to Homer," I said.

We reached the hotel and we went up to 5-F. Jane opened the door for us and I walked in, feeling that there should be signs around saying, "Achtung—Minen!"

Homer was waiting in the living room, with the early editions of the afternoon papers strewn around his chair. "Well," he said, "what's the verdict?"

"Senator Knott," I said.

"What about her?" Homer asked.

"She won the draw. She's going to be A.I. Mother Number One."

Homer started to rise, lost control of his legs, and sat down again, his mouth hanging open. "No!" he said when he could speak. "No! No! I won't do it, Steve. I won't have anything to do with this any more. Why she's the worst—the absolute worst—I'm going away right now." He got to his feet, and started for the door.

"Now wait a minute, Homer," I pleaded, clinging to his arm. "Wait a minute and let me tell you something." He was hard to stop as a telegraph pole that wants to go somewhere, but I slowed him down before he reached the door. "Homer," I said, "there are a lot of things to consider—an awful lot!"

I led him back to his chair, and he sat down and he put his head in his hands. Every few seconds he'd shake his head and pull his hair. "Homer," I said, "what is to be will be. It was all done fair and square, and you can bet that the President didn't want to pull her number out of the goldfish bowl because he doesn't like her any better than you do or I do. But this is a democracy, Homer, and that's the way we have to do things."

"It is a democracy for everyone except me," Homer protested. "I've got a hundred and forty million dictators sitting on my neck and I don't like it and I'm going away."

"It isn't as bad as you think," I told him, and motioned to Marge and told her to quick bring some liquor. "It could be much worse, Homer. Suppose you had to marry her and live with her? But you don't. You don't even have to see her. Actually, it doesn't make any difference to you whether she is number one or number eleven million eight hundred thousand six hundred and forty-two, now does it?"

"It makes a difference that she has a number at all," Homer said. "Imagine, when she has a child that will be my child too!"

"Well, all your children are bound to look pretty much alike, you know, Homer," I argued. "As a matter of fact you probably won't be able to tell one from the other in a few years."

"I've thought of that too," Homer replied, "and believe me I don't like it."

Marge brought drinks. Her hand was unsteady when she gave them to us. I remembered that Marge liked Homer, and she always felt she had a personal stake in him. "Now drink your drink and let's talk this over sensibly," I said.

"That's another thing I don't like," Homer went on stubbornly. "How would you like to go out on the street and everyone would have the same face and all of them would be like yours?"

"Well," I admitted, "I think it would be confusing, but at the same time that just illustrates how impersonal this matter has got to be to you."

Homer drew a deep breath, and drank his highball without taking his glass from his lips and just at that moment Gableman came in, followed by Abel Pumphrey, and both of them looked fresh and happy. Pumphrey grabbed Homer's hand and began to pump it and said, "Well, well, now we're on our way, aren't we, Homer? The worst is over, and there's all clear sailing ahead."

"That's what you think!" Homer said. "The worst is just beginning."

"No, you mustn't feel like that," said Mr. Pumphrey. "My boy, it was almost a miracle, having Senator Knott become A.I. Mother Number One. Almost a miracle! There can't be any criticism of N.R.P. about that pick—no, sir. It shows that the Administration is absolutely unbiased, allowing a member of the opposition to win the draw. And the Senate will like it, too. They'll all be proud to have one of their members become a mother."

Homer could not speak. I forced another drink into his hand.

Gableman showed a mouth full of rotting teeth in a wide grin. "Senator Knott is down in the lobby right now," he said. "She's coming up in just a moment to pose with you. She is an extremely attractive woman, isn't she, Homer? Even if she did cause us a little trouble some time ago, I don't think the President could have made a luckier choice, that is, from the political standpoint."

Homer choked on his drink and gasped, "Did you say she was coming up here?"

"Yes, just as soon as all the photographers and newsreel men arrive," said Gableman.

Suddenly Homer relaxed, in the manner of a fighter loosening up in his corner. "If she comes in here," he said, very softly, "I'll strangle her."

"You'll what?" said Abel Pumphrey, the veins jumping up from under his Herbert Hoover collar.

"I'll tear her to pieces and throw her up for grabs," Homer said, "like this." He extended his long arms and showed how.

I decided it was time to intervene. "Gentlemen," I said, "Mr. Adam is overwrought. He has been unnerved by the strain. I think you had better excuse him. You had better go on downstairs and tell

Senator Knott that Mr. Adam is sorry, because if she comes up here I really do think he will slap her around." I led them to the door, and got them outside.

"What's wrong with him?" Gableman asked. "Has he gone nuts?"

"My gracious," said Abel Pumphrey, "I never realized he was so temperamental. Why, he acts as if he thought he was the biggest man in N.R.P.! If anyone should have retained a grudge because of what Senator Knott said in the Senate, it should have been me. But I took it in my stride, and now I welcome Senator Knott as the ideal American A.I. mother. She has beauty, brains, and, ah, money. What more can Adam want, particularly when he doesn't have to actually, ah, to actually have any connubial contact with her."

"I think it's a little personal," said Gableman. "I'll always figure that Adam and that actress had a good deal more in common than archeology."

"I would watch him closely," Abel Pumphrey advised. "Very closely indeed. I simply don't understand him. I don't understand him at all."

Homer was still in his chair in the living room. "Well, I got rid of them," I told him.

"Thanks, Steve, but I really don't think I'll go through with it." He spoke very quietly, calm as a banker who has reached a decision not to make a questionable loan.

"I'll tell you frankly, Homer, I don't think there's much of a chance that Fay Knott will produce a baby anyway. She was married a couple of times, and nothing happened. When her second husband died, people said he froze to death."

"It is the principle of the thing," Homer said.

"That's exactly it—a matter of principle," I argued. "Is it right for any one man to put himself in the place of God, and condemn the world to slow death? You don't want to be in that position, do you?"

"I'm not putting myself in that position," Homer said. "I just don't want to have anything to do with that woman."

Marge sat on the edge of his chair, her long, sleek legs swinging, and ran her fingers through Homer's hair. It was the first time I had ever seen her touch another man like that, and I found that whatever I had to say had gone from my lips. "Think of the other women, Homer," Marge said. "Think of me and all the other women who will just curl up and die inside if they lose hope. You know, you're the hope of every woman, Homer—even those you'll never be able to satisfy."

Homer didn't answer. He kept his eyes on the floor. I knew he was thinking. I thought, I guess Marge put it over all right, and then I said, "We'll go down to the lab about noon tomorrow, Homer. We'll take it easy until then. Now buck up. It isn't really going to be as bad as you think. For the time being you're going to have a very easy program, and every day they don't need you in the lab we'll go to the races. You like the races, don't you?"

Presently Jane Zitter came in. She had been getting the latest bulletins from the Capitol on her bedroom radio. She was flushed with what I presume was a vicarious maternal instinct, and she began to recite the list of those fortunate enough to be drawn in the first group after Fay Knott. There was a National Committeewoman from California, the winner of last year's Atlantic City beauty contest, several childless widows of veterans, the wife of a railway president, and the granddaughter of a Vanderbilt.

"You see," I told Homer, "you should think of those people, instead of Knott. Think of how disappointed they would be if anything happened."

He nodded. I sighed. I thought my battle was won. I began to think of plans. Marge and I would take a sea voyage to Honolulu, or perhaps to Rio. The world would be a good place to live in again. Eventually, I might even allow Marge to persuade me to okay an A.I. baby. The telephone rang, Homer unfolded and answered it, and presently he began his ritual of yeses, noes, and grunts that showed The Frame was on the other end. I mentally kicked myself for not having asked the FBI to put a tap on our phone. I'd have given anything to have known what The Frame was telling Homer, but his face was immobile and unrevealing.

That night we played bridge, and at nine o'clock I flicked on the wall radio, and who should be there but Gabriel Heatter. "Oh, there's good news tonight," he said like the peal of an organ. "Yes, there's good news tonight. Dare I say it? Yes, I think I will dare say it. Mankind marches on! Tomorrow there begins the greatest experiment in all history. Will it succeed? Will it fail? It must succeed! Yes, everyone in the sound of my voice knows that. It must succeed!"

"You see what honest Gabe says," I told Homer.

"And Heatter predicts that it will succeed," Heatter said. "Heatter wants you to remember that Heatter predicted the end of Hitler—and Mussolini. And now Heatter predicts it will succeed! Nine months from tomorrow we will all breathe easy again! Nine months from tomorrow that fine and inspiring example of American womanhood, Senator Fay Sumner Knott, will again lift aloft the glorious torch of motherhood. Nine months from tomorrow there will be a miracle—a baby will be born!"

Homer smiled. I didn't like the way he smiled. "What are you thinking, Homer?" I asked.

"Oh, nothing," Homer replied. "Nothing at all, really."

Heatter insidiously switched from a description of Homer's hair, to the need of all men for hair tonic, and I shut him off. "What do you think of honest Gabe?" I asked Homer, feeling uneasy about that smile.

"I like to listen to him," Homer replied. "He is so optimistic."

"Yes," Jane agreed. "During the Battle of the Bulge I don't know how I could have carried on without Heatter."

"I don't think he's a newscaster at all," I said. "I think he's a chanter in a choir. But I like to listen to him, as Homer does, because he is so optimistic. I feel that so long as Heatter and his partner, God, have everything in hand, I don't have to worry."

Homer yawned. "If you'll excuse me," he said, "I think I'll go to bed. I've got a hard day ahead, you know."

I told him I thought that was a splendid idea, and he was to forget all his worries. "You just go into this as if it was a business," I said. "The laboratory will be your office, and on certain days you have to go to the office. All the rest of the time you will be free. Just consider yourself a capitalist who only has to go to the office two or three times a week, and spend an hour or two. You know, it isn't so bad, Homer, when you look at it that way."

Homer smiled as if nothing were funny. "Good night," he said. "Good night."

Jane Zitter went to bed, and that left Marge and me. "Well, I guess that flap is over," I said. I began to talk about Honolulu, and Rio, and the gaudy beauty of Sydney harbor, and the minaret-speared moon rising over old Stambul, and the comparative stenches of Naples, Venice, and Cairo.

Marge listened, placid and enigmatic as a lovely model in a department store window. "Do you really believe it?" she said finally. "Do you really believe that anything like that is going to happen, ever again? I don't think you really believe it. I think you're just whistling to keep up your courage."

"Certainly I believe it," I protested. "By the middle of summer everything will be back to normal, including us. We'll have a glorious time."

"Would you like to know what I think?" Marge asked.

"What do you think?"

"I think that if Kay Sumner Knott has a baby you will be able to call it an immaculate conception."

"You're a cynic, like J.C. Pogey."

"We'll see."

We kept on arguing until long after midnight, with Marge insisting that things wouldn't work out right. She said she didn't like the way Homer was acting, and I said I didn't either but I wasn't going to do anything rash that would upset him. She said she had a premonition, and I said that I didn't believe in premonitions or ghosts or poltergeists. She said I was a stubborn double-dyed jackass and I said she was a neurotic old woman who probably looked under the bed every night when I wasn't home. She reminded me of all the times she had been right and I had been wrong, and I said that just as many times I had been right and she had been wrong, but I didn't keep all those times in a catalogue, the way she did, because it would embarrass her. She said I could sleep in my own bed, and I said that was fine with me, and I did.

When I awoke Marge was sitting on the edge of the bed, looking at me. She leaned over and kissed me and said, "I'll say I'm sorry if you'll say you're sorry."

"I'm sorry," I said.

"It's a dream of a morning," she said. "It's spring. Birds and everything." Some robins were trying out their voices, and the sun was beating in through the open window, and the breeze from the park smelled of growing things.

It was ten o'clock. We put on our robes and went into the living room and picked up the morning papers. "I'm running up a little breakfast," Jane called from the kitchenette. "How do you want your eggs?"

"Poached, honey," I yelled back. "Marge too. Where's Homer?"

"Oh, he went out for a walk in the park," Jane said.

"He did? How long ago?"

"He went out at nine. Said he'd be back for breakfast. Isn't it a glorious morning?"

"Perfect. How did he look?"

"I've never seen him look better. He absolutely sparkled. He looked like a schoolboy going out to buy candy for his first date."

"That's fine," I said. Marge looked at me, her head cocked on one side. "Yes, isn't it," she agreed.

"The eggs will be ready in two minutes," Jane yelled.

I picked up the *Post* and glanced from headline to headline. No matter how much I concentrated, I couldn't retain a word or a phrase. "Hadn't you better go out and find Homer?" Marge suggested sweetly.

"Oh, I don't think so," I said. "He might be on any path in Rock Creek Park, and we'd just miss each other. Anyway, he'll be right back."

"Do you think so, dear?"

"What's wrong with Homer taking a walk in the park? He's often taken a walk in the park."

"There's nothing wrong with it, dear, so long as he comes back."

Jane brought a plate and put it on my lap. Two eggs, nestling on buttered toast, stared at me like accusing yellow eyes. Suddenly I wasn't hungry. I put the plate aside. "Don't you think you had better go out and find him now, dear?" Marge suggested again. I didn't like the way she said "dear." It was like a knife blade sliding across my throat. I didn't like anything about this morning. I felt that the sun, the birds, the grass and the buds were all laughing at me. I noticed that Jane was watching me, and that little beads of perspiration were standing out on her face, and that her fingers were tightly intertwined.

I got up and said, "Yes, I think I'd better go out and find him." I dressed in a hurry. It didn't seem necessary to put on a tie.

Out in front of the hotel I looked carefully up and down the street. Wouldn't it be smarter, I thought, just to wait here for him? There were a dozen roads and pathways that led into Rock Creek Park, in the space of a few blocks, and he might be on any one of them. I tried waiting. I waited for five minutes. Any second, now, he will turn up. Any second I will see that red head bobbing along. I started walking toward Connecticut Avenue, changed my mind, and went in the other direction. Back of the hotel a road curved through the park, and I found myself hurrying down this road. I walked perhaps a half-mile before I stopped. This is stupid, I told myself. This is utterly stupid. He's probably back at the hotel right now, and Jane and Marge are laughing at me.

I walked back to the hotel. "Did you see Mr. Adam come in?" I asked the doorman.

"No, Mr. Smith. I saw him go out, earlier, but I haven't seen him come in."

"What did he do when he went out?"

"I don't think I noticed. He just walked away."

"Did he meet anybody?"

"Let me see. No, he didn't meet anybody. He just walked away. Of course, Mr. Smith, he might have come back through one of the other entrances. Maybe he came in through the terrace, and the swimming pool. If he went walking in the park, that's the quickest way back, you know."

"Oh, certainly," I said. "Thanks." Naturally, if he went walking in the park, he'd return through the back. He'd probably come back while I waited outside. If he came through the back, the desk clerk would probably have seen him.

I went over to the desk and asked the clerk if he had seen Mr. Adam this morning.

"Why yes, Mr. Smith," he said. "I saw him about nine. He left an envelope for you. He said you'd be down later to pick it up." He reached into a letter box and brought out an envelope and handed it to me just as if it were an ordinary envelope.

"Thanks," I said. I suppose I smiled. People always smile when the desk clerk hands them an envelope, even when it's an eviction notice, or an advertisement, or a bill. I put it in my pocket, and my legs carried me to the elevator. I said, "Five, please," as if nothing had happened.

The operator said, "Aren't you feeling well, Mr. Smith?"

"Oh, not so good," I said. "Not so bad but not so good."

I found myself standing in front of the door to 5-F. I thought, maybe it's only a note saying he'll be a little late, and I'm making a fool of myself. I thought, maybe I'd better open it here before I go in. I pulled it out of my pocket and looked at it. It was a hotel envelope and on the face of it was scrawled, *Steve Smith.* That didn't tell me anything. I thought, if he's running away, the quicker I find out about it the better. I started to open it and then put it back in my pocket. You're yellow, I told myself. I took it out of my pocket again. I opened the door and walked into 5-F.

"Well?" Marge asked.

"He didn't come back?" I said. She didn't answer. "He left a— there was a letter or something down at the desk." I tried to open it, but I didn't seem to be making any progress.

"Let me have it!" Marge demanded. She took the envelope from me, and slid a sharp thumbnail under the flap and it popped open with no trouble at all. Inside was a single sheet of paper, with writing on both sides. She spread it out on the table, and I read it over her shoulder. Homer had written:

Dear Steve,

Please consider this my resignation from N.R.P. Under the Constitution and by other laws I have got as much right to resign as anyone else, and I resign, as of now.

I hate to do it, because I know it will get you into trouble. You have been a good friend, and believe me if it gets you into trouble I am sorry, but I am sure you can get out of it.

I might as well tell you, because you will find out soon enough. I am going away with Kathy. We are going away and we are not coming back. I tried my best to do my duty, and I wouldn't have minded so much if Senator Knott hadn't been picked as Mother Number One. That was too much. And as Kathy pointed out to me, the first A.I. child might very well inherit all the bad traits of both Senator Knott and me, and I don't feel that we have the right to impose any such thing upon the world.

I am inclined to agree with Mr. Pogey that the world is, and by rights ought to be, extinct. And so long as it is going to be extinct, why prolong the agony?

I am sorry to leave Mary Ellen and little Eleanor, but there is money enough to care for them. I think Mary Ellen will understand that my only chance for happiness is to resign and go away with Kathy. She is the only one who has the courage to help me. So, goodbye, Steve.

Homer.

P.S. Give my love to Marge, and tell Jane goodbye for me.

I picked up the telephone. "Who are you going to call?" Marge asked.

"I have had it!" I told her. I think I spoke without undue passion, and with determination. "I have had it, and I am going to call the airport, and we will get on a plane to New York right away. We'll retire to Smith Field and pretend none of it happened."

Marge took the telephone out of my hand and slammed it on its cradle. "Oh, no you're not!" she told me. "You can't! You're responsible, Steve. If you run out, now, I'll leave you. I swear it. I'll leave you flat."

Jane was reading Homer's note. She finished it, it fluttered in her hand, and she quietly slid to the floor. "Do you see what you've done?" Marge said. "She's fainted. Get a wet towel, you dope, and start thinking!"

CHAPTER 11

My every instinct warned me to get out of that hotel fast, and keep going, but since I could not do this, there were obvious steps to be taken. First I called the N.R.P., and asked for Abel Pumphrey. His secretary answered, and asked who was calling and I told her and she said, "Couldn't you call back a little later, Mr. Smith. Mr. Pumphrey is very busy right now."

I said it was urgent, and she said Mr. Pumphrey had said he did not want to be disturbed, because he was working on his radio script with Mr. Gableman. "You know he's speaking tonight on a national hookup," she said, "on the beginning of A.I."

"This will concern his speech," I said, "very vitally."

"In that case," she said, "I'd better put you through."

"Who's this?" Pumphrey's voice said. "Oh, it's you, Smith. I'm terribly busy right now, couldn't you—"

"Homer Adam," I said, "has run away."

There was a choking sound at the other end of the line, and then, "I don't think I understood you, Smith—Steve—did you say—"

"Homer Adam has run away. He has gone. He has vanished."

There were loud, strange noises on the other end of the line, and disconnected words and phrases, but they were not coming from Abel Pumphrey.

"What's happening," Marge asked.

"I don't know. Sounds like the place was suddenly invaded by furniture movers."

I kept on saying hello, hello into the telephone, and after a number of minutes a voice on the other end said, "Hello, hello, is this Smith? Gableman. What did you do to Mr. Pumphrey?"

"What's wrong with him?"

"He's out cold. I think he's had a heart attack. We're sending him to the hospital."

"I told him about Homer Adam. He just resigned. He ran away. He's gone."

"Oh! Oh, no!" Gableman groaned as if he had a stomach-ache, and then he said, "I'll be right over. Don't do anything until I get there."

"I'm going to call the FBI," I said. "I have to. Sorry about Pumphrey."

"My gosh, when this gets out! Do you think we can find him in a hurry?"

"I don't know. I don't know whether we'll ever find him."

"Well, tell the FBI not to make it public until they have to, because if it's made public we'll all be ruined, and we might find him." He hung up.

Marge said, "That was a peculiar conversation. What happened?"

"Oh, Pumphrey had a heart attack, and Gableman is coming over."

"If he dies," Marge said, "you'll be a murderer!"

I asked the operator for the FBI, and then I told Marge that if she ever said another thing like that I would resign, like Homer, and go away, and if Pumphrey had a bad heart, and was fated to pass out on this lovely spring morning, then I couldn't be blamed. Marge began to sniffle, and Jane, now recovered, put her arm around her shoulder, and I felt like a heel.

I got through to Inspector Root, at the FBI. Tex Root is a spare little man, quick and wiry as a blacksnake whip. Nothing ever surprises him, because usually he keeps about two thoughts ahead of everyone else. I had gone to Root when I needed a dossier on The Frame, and now when I told him about Homer vanishing he said, "Did that gal get him?"

"It looks that way," I said.

"I thought she might," he said. "Now don't get yourself into an uproar. This may not be as bad as it looks. I guess you want to keep it quiet, heh?"

"It might prevent a number of lynchings and murders and I don't know what else."

"So it might," Tex Root agreed. I knew he would be smiling. "All right, we won't put out a public alarm—not yet. You're positive he's with the Riddell woman?"

"He left a note."

"Okay, we'll put special agents on the railroads, and air lines, and air charter ships, and bus lines—but I'm pretty sure she's too smart to use them. And I'll be up in five minutes."

Gableman arrived first. He wasn't alone. With him was Klutz, bubbling incoherently with excitement and apprehension. "How's Pumphrey?" I greeted them, feeling guilty.

"His condition is undetermined," said Klutz. "It's awful, isn't it? Why, if anything happens to Mr. Pumphrey, there's no telling what the results might be. The whole organization might come to pieces. I don't see how he could be replaced, I really don't."

"Looks bad, all right," Gableman said. "There's already been so much talk about putting N.R.P. under Interior, or Public Health, that if something happened to Mr. Pumphrey such a switch might be inevitable. Of course, it wouldn't affect me personally. Interior has been after me to come over to them, and State wants me back, but we do have such a nice, tight little organization in N.R.P. that I'd hate to leave."

"So would I," said Klutz. "And the worst of it is I'd probably have to stay on until the last to supervise liquidation."

Gableman shook his head and sat down. "I just don't see how I can save this situation," he said. "If we don't find Adam immediately we won't be able to keep it quiet. As a matter of fact I don't know whether we'll be able to keep it quiet in any case. Colonel Phelps-Smythe is sure to hear about it, and he'll go running to the War Department, and there's no telling what they'll do."

Tex Root arrived. I was glad to see him. Not only did he look sane, but you knew that he would remain that way. I gave him Homer's note, and he read it aloud, twice, and then he said, "They can't get away with it."

"Why not?" I asked.

"Why, they're as conspicuous as, well, as if Joe Stalin and Winston Churchill were loose. More. Everywhere they go, they'll be recognized. Particularly since this is A.I. Day. Suppose they turned up in Kansas City? Somebody would say, 'Why, there's Mr. Adam! And The Frame! Why, he's supposed to be in Washington today, starting A.I.' And the heat would be on."

"That sounds logical," I admitted.

"It is logical," said Tex Root, "but only if we send out a general alarm. If we put out a general alarm the chances are we'd locate them in six hours."

Gableman started to pace the floor. "Yes, but can you imagine what would happen if it was broadcast that Mr. Adam had vanished? Why—" The vision of the consequences seemed to render him speechless.

"I can imagine," said Tex Root quietly. "It would be like Pearl Harbor, only worse. I think people would get killed. For instance, I think Kathy Riddell would probably get killed, and I think some of you people in N.R.P. would get killed, and those who didn't would wish they were dead. People feel very strongly about Homer Adam, and A.I. I know. I'm a married man. It was bad enough when people discovered that Adam was living with his wife. I don't know what they'd do if they learned he'd eloped with an actress."

"Exactly!" said Gableman. "There'd be chaos."

Tex Root thought it over, his neat, lean fingers tapping the arm of his chair. "However," he concluded, "it is the duty of the Bureau to find him, and as quickly as possible. I will treat it exactly as if it were a kidnaping. If Adam hasn't turned up by midnight, and our Special Agents haven't found any trace of him, we'll have to make it public."

"That's reasonable," I agreed. I sat down and gave him a fill-in on everything I knew about Homer Adam, and The Frame. Everything. When I got to the part about their mutual interest in Aztec archeology Root nodded. "It could be," he said, "that they're headed for Mexico. If they are, we'll soon know about it."

He called his office, and dictated additional instructions. "You see," he said, "we'll not only check up on every commercial service going to Mexico, but we'll check all private planes that might be chartered for such a flight."

I told him about The Frame's phone calls to Homer, and together we went to the hotel switchboard. One of the girls remembered that Miss Riddell had called the previous evening. It wasn't a long distance call. It was local. She didn't know from where. Usually, Miss Riddell's calls came from out of town. But they had been local for the past three days.

"That tells us something," Root said when we returned to 5-F. "She was here last night. Where does she stay when she's in Washington?" I told him and he called her hotel, but the hotel didn't know anything about Miss Riddell's being in the city. "She's been keeping under cover," he said. "Shows she planned this carefully. I don't think we'll find them by midnight. We may not find them for a long, long time. She's a very clever girl. Very."

The telephone rang and Jane Zitter answered it. "It's the N.R.P. laboratory," she said. "The doctors are ready for Mr. Adam. They've been waiting."

I had forgotten. It was past noon. "Tell them," I began, "tell them—what would you tell them, Gableman?"

"Oh," said Gableman. "Oh, Lord, please let me think. Tell them that Mr. Adam can't make it today."

"That's pretty lame," I said. "We've got to do better than that. And we'll certainly have to do better than that later in the day, or this evening, when Fay Sumner Knott calls and asks for her impregnation."

"Oh," Gableman groaned, "why did I ever leave the State Department? Nothing like this ever happened in the State Department."

"Hold the wire a moment, please," Jane said into the phone.

"Has anybody got any ideas?" I asked.

"Can't you think up an international complication?" Marge suggested.

"That's it!" said Gableman. "An international complication. Tell then that Mr. Adam cannot make it today, because of international complications. Tell them there are some things that have to be cleared before A.I. begins."

Jane told the laboratories. "What things will have to be cleared?" I asked. "We'll have to make this real."

"That's not hard," said Gableman. "I can think of a hundred things that have to be cleared. Why, we've got whole stacks of protests in our files. We just got a beaut from the Russians last night. They charge that Fay Sumner Knott has been unfriendly to the Soviet Union, and as a matter of fact they cannot find anyone on the whole list who is friendly to the Soviet Union, and they protest the whole thing. And the French are indignant, and so are the Chinese. They all claim that unless some priority is given to other countries, there isn't any guarantee that the United States isn't pursuing a unilateral policy."

"That ought to do it," I said, "at least temporarily. That will hold us until midnight, anyway."

"All right," Gableman agreed, "I'll go back to the office and fight a delaying action. But I want you to understand that if nothing has happened before midnight, I'm through. At midnight I'm going to leave the office and I will never return. Tomorrow you will find me with Interior."

Klutz said, rising, "Mr. Smith, if you had only taken my advice in the first place, and allowed Mr. Adam to operate under the aegis of a committee, with the War Department sharing responsibility, we wouldn't be in this mess. I'd like you to know that you have endangered my career, Mr. Smith."

I started to speak, but I thought better of it because Marge and Jane were there. Gableman and Klutz left, and I went into the kitchenette and found Tex Root spreading cheese on crackers. "If you're hungry," I suggested, "we can have lunch sent up."

"I'm not hungry," Tex said. "I was just thinking, and when I eat crackers I think best."

"And what are you thinking?" I asked.

"I was just thinking it's just like my wife said. You get a shortage of anything, and people start to make a black market out of it."

"You don't mean that The Frame grabbed Homer for a black market in babies?"

"Well, that's what my wife would say, right away. It would be practically instinctive. But I'm not sure of it. There may be other motives, besides selling stuff on the black market, but they're hard to find."

I could imagine The Frame as being a lot of things, but somehow she didn't strike me as being avaricious for money. I said, "I think you're being cynical."

"Oh, you do? Well, turn on the radio."

"What's the radio got to do with it?"

Tex Root bit off half a cracker, munched it, and then stuffed the other half in his mouth. In a muffled voice he said, "Homer Adam affects the stock market, doesn't he?"

"Sure," I replied. "When Adam's well, stocks are up. When they're down, it's a pretty good sign that either Adam is sick, or N.R.P. is in trouble."

"And so far as the public knows, this is a big day—a boom day—isn't it?"

"Certainly. This is A.I. Day."

"And stocks should go up?"

"Oh, I suppose so. Moderately perhaps. After all, A.I. Day has been pretty well discounted by the professional traders."

"What would you think if you turned on the radio and found stocks had collapsed?"

I thought this over. "If it was really a general collapse, it could only mean that war had started or the insiders thought Adam was ended."

"All right," said Tex Root, "I dare you to turn on the radio."

I turned it on. It played music, and then a girl sang a little ditty about how to keep moths out of closets, and then the National Association of Industry announced it was presenting Mr. Henry Mullet, Jr., on the air, to give his version of the news, "completely uncensored and as he sees it."

"Now watch," said Tex Root. Sure enough, Mr. Henry Mullet, Jr., started off by stating that the stock market had collapsed, but on its face, with heavy selling inspired by rumors from Washington. He didn't say what the rumors were.

"Now you see why I'm cynical," said Tex Root. "You think you can keep it a secret about Homer Adam disappearing, but so long as more than one person knows about it, it's no secret. And everybody who finds out about it, plays it smart. They sell humanity short."

I didn't like the phrase about selling humanity short, and said so. He said I ought to learn to be a realist. He reminded me that during the war everyone made money out of ships and airplanes except the fellows who died in them, and that after the war everyone made money out of houses except the people who needed them for living. I said I didn't see what that had to do with black markets, and he said it illustrated the economics of shortages. He said it showed there were other reasons why The Frame might want to grab Homer Adam besides the ones we'd already considered.

The telephone kept ringing, and every time it rang I hoped it would be for Tex Root, but it never was.

Klutz called to tell me that Mr. Pumphrey was better, and in fact out of danger. His high blood pressure had boiled over, and the doctors advised him to take a month off, but he would live.

Gableman called to say that he had put out a release announcing that A.I. Day was postponed twenty-four hours, but that it had not been well received, and the press wanted to know specifically why. "This business of international complications," he explained, "is getting hard to work. The press associations always cable Moscow, and Moscow never knows what is up and issues a denial, and then the State Department gets huffy and denies having received the denial. One of these days that sort of thing will get me in bad. That is why I would rather work for Interior."

Dinnertime went by. Tex Root and Marge and Jane devoured chicken sandwiches and drank milk, but I wasn't feeling hungry. Midnight was getting no further away, and I was having visions. Very shortly I would be the most unpopular man in the world. I was the man on the spot. There wasn't anything that could save me. There was no evading it. I kept telling myself that during a crisis like this a man's viewpoint becomes distorted, and everything appears worse than it actually is. Then Danny Williams called from the White House and I discovered that things can actually be as bad as they seem.

"The President," Danny said, "is having a conniption fit. I don't blame him. Why weren't we notified?"

"I thought somebody in the office would tell him," I apologized. It didn't sound right. I knew, and Danny knew, that no one in N.R.P. would want to be a bearer of black news.

"We didn't know a damned thing about it until the War Department called."

"Oh, do they know about it?"

"Certainly they know about it. Everyone in Washington knew about it, except the President. He wants your scalp, but I told him to wait. I hear the FBI has given you a midnight deadline."

"That's right, and it doesn't look good."

"Well, if he's not back by midnight the War Department is going to take over. They're drawing up an executive order now. This is serious, Steve."

"I know."

"I'm sorry, Steve, but that's the way it has to be."

I said okay, and hung up. I felt tired. "We're all washed up," I told Marge. "Your husband is in disgrace. You might as well start packing."

"Says who?" she asked, trying to sound insouciant.

"Says the President of the United States."

"Oh," she said in a small voice. "Oh, I'm so sorry for you, Steve. What'll they do to you?"

"Officially, nothing. Unofficially, I don't even want to guess. When you consider what the American public did to a baseball player who failed to touch second base, and a football player who once ran the wrong way, I can't even imagine what they'll do to me."

Gableman called again, to say that Fay Sumner Knott was behaving like a bride whose husband was out with another woman on the first night of the wedding. "I just want to tell you," he said, "that I'm cleaning out my desk and moving. I don't want to have any part of what is going to happen."

At ten o'clock Tex Root called the FBI. His Special Agents hadn't developed even a likely lead. After Kathy Riddell arrived in Washington four days before, she had simply dropped into a void, just as Homer Adam had vanished when he walked into the carefully manicured woods of Rock Creek Park. "Why wait?" I suggested. "Why not blow off the lid now? She probably picked him up in a car, and the longer we wait to broadcast the news, the further away they'll be."

Tex Root picked up a magazine. "No," he decided. "I said twelve and we'll wait until twelve. Anyway, the local police can't do much in the dark."

"The local police?"

"Yes. They'll have to search the park, and drag the creek. That's normal procedure."

"You mean, you think he might be——murdered?"

Root looked up from his magazine. "Well, that's a possibility, isn't it?"

Jane began to cry. She had been sitting in her chair, very quietly, and at first she tried to hide her tears, but then the sounds escaped her, and finally she could no longer hold back the steady sobs that shook her body like a great, unseen hand. Marge put an arm around her, and got her into a bedroom. Marge came back and said she hoped they wouldn't need a doctor, but unless Jane calmed down in a few minutes we'd have to call one. "What's the trouble with her?" Root asked.

"She doesn't like Kathy Riddell. She's afraid of her. She thinks she's a bad woman. And Jane is very fond of Homer."

"I don't think Kathy is so bad," I said. I knew when I said it that it was a final and a very weak defense against the fears that had been trying to burst into my consciousness. I remembered, again, how she had looked at the airport, and how I had been chilled by that glimpse of fanaticism. "Tex," I said finally, "would you think I was crazy if I suggested that perhaps Kathy Riddell planned to do away with Homer Adam? Would you think I was crazy if I suggested that this isn't as simple as Homer getting disgusted, and running off with her because he believes he loves her? I mean, in view of your report on her patriotism and loyalty?"

"What are you getting at?" he asked.

"Well suppose—now just suppose—that there was a group of scientists who wanted to murder not Homer Adam, but civilization? Suppose the Mississippi explosion wasn't an accident at all. Suppose it was planned, and Homer's escape upset the plan. So to carry out their plans completely, they have to block A.I., and that means doing away with Homer."

"That's horrible!" said Marge. "It makes my spine crawl. I'm frightened."

The lines seemed to deepen in Tex Root's thin face. "I can imagine one crazy nuclear physicist," he said, "but not a whole bunch of them. As a class, they are about the sanest people I know. And remember that I worked on Manhattan Project security, and I know them pretty well."

"Yes," I said. "You're right."

"Besides, Kathy Riddell lost her fiancé when Mississippi blew up."

"Sure, forget I ever mentioned it. I guess my thinking is pretty wild."

"No, I'm not going to forget it," Tex Root said. "This is a very peculiar world, and the most peculiar thing in it is the human mind. Now if Kathy Riddell was involved in any such plot, she wouldn't be the brains behind it, now would she? She was a pretty small cog in the development of fission, no more important than Jane Zitter is to N.R.P. But she would be a useful tool for a particular job."

"Yes," I agreed. "Her equipment for seduction is probably unrivalled."

"All right. Now we're getting somewhere. Who would be her

bosses?" Root ticked them off on his fingers as he named them. "Logically, there's her father, Professor Ruppe from the University of Chicago. There are Canby and Welles, in Berkeley. She worked with both of them. And of course there's the old master, Felix Pell, in New York."

"He's the one I don't like," I said. "To me he looks like a movie villain."

Tex Root laughed. "So to you he looks like a villain! Why, he's one of the sweetest old men I ever met in my life! And two generations of graduates at Columbia will tell you the same thing. He's a leader in practically every civilized movement that comes out of New York City, he's contributed most of his income to charities—I think he even gave away his Nobel prize money—and besides he's got five children and I don't know how many grandchildren."

"Still he looks like a villain."

Root moved out of his chair and picked up the phone at my elbow. "We'll give it a check," he said. "We'll soon know." He put in calls for Professor Ruppe, in Chicago, and Dr. Pell, in New York. He got through to Chicago almost instantly. There was a good deal of talking, but not with Professor Ruppe, and he put down the telephone and said, "Ruppe isn't in. He's in Washington. He can be reached through the Carnegie Institute. Well, that's interesting, but that's all."

Then the New York call went through, and Root talked, politely, for a few moments, and asked questions. When he finished he put the telephone down gently, almost reverently, as if it were a delicate and noble instrument. "I can't believe it," he said, in a soft voice that retained just a touch of drawl. "I can hardly believe it! Why old Dr. Pell is in Washington, too. He's staying at the home of Peter Pflaum. Pflaum runs Carnegie's cyclotron."

I snatched the phone book and fingered my way into the P's. Pflaum lived on Rapidan Place, N.W. It is a little, recently created street hardly two blocks long. It is a ten minute walk from the hotel, and it runs just to the edge of the park. "How beautifully simple," I said. "He just walked out of the hotel, crossed the park, and into their house—right into their hands. He was blind as an ant that follows a trail of sugar into the flypaper. The poor guy!"

"Now wait a minute," Root said. "Up to now this is just coincidence. We may be way off."

"Do you believe it?"

"I don't believe anything until I see it. But let's get started. I've got my car parked outside." He reached for his topcoat, and the phone tinkled again and Marge answered and said it was for Inspector Root.

"Damn," Root said, and picked up the telephone, buttoning his topcoat with his free hand. "Yes, Colonel," he said, and after that all I could catch were snatches of conversation. "I don't think it's necessary . . . but that's hardly evidence . . . up to now I don't find anything to make me see spies . . . certainly I realize the War Department is responsible for security, but so is the FBI . . . all right, Colonel, it's all yours at twelve o'clock, but until then I'll use my own judgment."

"What's up?" I asked.

"That was your pal Phelps-Smythe. He wants me to hold you."

"Hold me?" My insides wrapped themselves into a tight little knot. "For what?"

"Now don't worry. The way he puts it is hold you for your own protection, but actually he's convinced the whole thing is a Communist plot. G-2 has made a check on your secretary, Jane Zitter, and they've discovered she was on a Dies Committee list some years ago. It seems she got literature from the League for Peace and Democracy. I told him it could be but I didn't see how that made you a Communist, and he said look what happened in Canada, and this smelled like the same thing, and he wants me to hold you."

"So are you holding me?"

"He is not a Communist!" Marge protested. "He makes too

much money to be a Communist, and not enough to be a capitalist, and besides he's too lazy."

"Thank you, dear," I told her. "I think that is a remarkable defense."

"Come on, let's get out of here," said Root. "If we stay here any longer I'll be wacky as the rest of you people."

And we left.

CHAPTER 12

The drive across the park didn't take more than five minutes, but in five minutes you can have a lot of nightmares. I wish I'd never seen the Frankenstein pictures. I could imagine finding Homer Adam in the attic, strapped to all kinds of intricate and horrid machines. And I could imagine our finding a few charred bones in the basement. I could also imagine our discovering that he had been dissolved in acid, and dispatched to heaven via the bathtub drain. But the worst thing I could imagine was that these men, being handy with an atom, would simply disintegrate him without trace. No, that wasn't quite the worst thing. The absolute worst was that we wouldn't find Homer or Kathy at all.

When we came out of the park, and turned into Rapidan, Tex Root switched off our lights, and eased his sedan to the curb. We got out, he glanced at a house number, and said, "That will be it down the street there—the one with the lights."

It was a large house of modern, undistinguished architecture, set within gracious grounds. It was an ample house that spoke of guest rooms and library, of a den and a play room, and the square of poplars behind it probably shielded a tennis court. It was a house within which you would expect to find a retired senator, or a justice of the District of Columbia courts, or a lobbyist for steel or rubber, or a college chancellor, or perhaps a scientist with an independent income, like Peter Pflaum. Both floors were lighted, but on the lower floor the Venetian blinds were down, and drawn so that a narrow grid of light escaped.

"Well," I said, as we walked up the path to the door, "what do we do now?"

"We ring," said Tex Root, and he rang. He waited a moment, and he rang again, holding his thumb against the opalescent button. He held his thumb there until the door opened. It opened only a few inches.

There was a man's face in the opening, a broad, pleasant, middle-aged face wearing glasses. "Yes?" the man said.

"Are you Mr. Pflaum?" Root said.

"Yes, I'm Pflaum. But I'm very busy right now. We're having a little conference here. I don't believe I know you, but if you care to see me you will find me in my office any time after ten o'clock tomorrow."

"I'm really sorry to disturb you, Mr. Pflaum," Root said, "but I'm afraid I must see you now. I'm from the FBI."

Pflaum's polite smile set, as if it were there to stay. "Couldn't you see me tomorrow? I can't imagine what the FBI—"

"No, Mr. Pflaum, I couldn't. I want to apologize in advance, but I have to come in."

Pflaum started to say something more, but he looked at Root's face, and what he saw there told him it was useless. His smile disappeared, and he opened the door, and he said, "What is it you want?" but he said it as if he knew what we wanted.

"We're looking for Mr. Adam," Root said.

"How on earth—how on earth did you know?"

Root didn't answer. He pushed past Pflaum, and I followed him. I realized that while we waited outside I had heard voices, but that when we entered, they stopped.

"Where is he?" Root demanded, as we walked down the hall. I saw that Pflaum was following us. "In there," he said, "that doorway on the right."

I don't know what I expected to see when I walked into the Pflaum library, except I knew I would see Homer Adam. I suppose I expected he would be bound and gagged, or perhaps plain dead. But whatever it was I expected, it wasn't what I saw. I think that I was as surprised at seeing Homer and Kathy, as they were at seeing me.

Unlike most libraries, this one was constructed for reading and research. The bookshelves covered the walls, and reached from the floor to the ceiling. There was a mobile stepladder in a corner, and in another corner an enormous desk, stacked with books, pamphlets, and clippings. Pflaum must have been sitting at this desk, when we rang, for it was the only unoccupied chair in the room.

In a little semi-circle, chairs facing the desk, were Pell, a tall man with a Vandyke who I felt would be Professor Ruppe, and a much younger man whom I did not recognize. In another chair sat The Frame, a cigarette almost, but not quite, touching her parted lips. Closest to the desk, his ungainly hands gripping the arms of his chair, was Homer Adam. He looked bewildered, but hardly more bewildered than usual.

I knew that I should say something, but I felt puzzled, and out of place, as if I had invaded a family conference. Except for the presence of Homer, that was the way it seemed. "Hadn't I better get some chairs for you gentlemen?" Pflaum said incongruously. "Don't you want to sit down?"

I didn't see Root take the gun out of his shoulder holster, but suddenly there it was, in his hand, a Smith and Wesson magnum, and I remember wondering how such a small man could conceal such a cannon on his person without it being noticeable. "Don't move!" Root said, in a low voice but firmly. "I know this is an obsolete type of weapon, not fit for wiping out whole populations, but it will blow a hole through you, big as your arm, and that's exactly what I'm going to do if anyone moves."

Somehow, this relieved the tension. It put us all back in our proper places. We weren't guests any more. We were there to save Homer Adam.

"But I don't understand," said Pflaum, "how in the world you ever guessed—"

"You don't have to understand," Root said. "But there are a lot of things that I'll have to understand."

"Now just a moment," said Pell, his massive head jerking on his scrawny neck. "Nobody here has committed any crime, and I think it's an outrage for you to come in here like this and threaten us with that weapon as if we were gangsters. After all, we're all associates of the National Research Council."

"Isn't kidnaping a crime any more?" said Root.

"There has been no kidnaping," Pell protested. "Mr. Adam came here voluntarily, and we were just having a little discussion concerning some most important matters."

Homer tried to rise, but whenever Homer tried to get out of a deep chair it was a nerve-racking struggle, particularly when the situation was critical, for at those times his legs refused to co-ordinate. "Sit down, Homer," I told him. "Sure, he came here voluntarily, but I'll bet this is the last place he expected to be. Isn't that right, Homer?"

"Steve," he began. "Steve, I'm terribly sorry. I'm not quite sure what's happening."

"Naturally he's not sure what's happening," I said. "He thinks he is escaping from the N.R.P.—for which I can't blame him much— and eloping with The Frame here, for which I don't blame him much either, and what happens? He finds himself locked up with a bunch of crazy professors. Say, what's your name?" I asked the young man whose name I didn't know.

"I'm John Canby, from the University of California," he said, starting to rise. Root's gun waved him back into his chair.

I said, "It's certainly a nice, cozy little rendezvous, isn't it? What were they up to, Homer? What were they going to do to you?"

"I don't know," Homer replied. "I really don't understand it at all. I didn't know it was supposed to be this way. The way I understood it, Kathy and I were to stay here for a few days, and then we were to drive to Mexico."

"You are so damn innocent, Homer," I said. "You're just like a steer being led into the stockyards. Well, if you don't know what was going to happen to you, I'll enlighten you. This pack of respectable, scientific ghouls was going to eliminate you. And I'll tell you why, Homer. They don't like the human race. They want to give the world back to the lizards."

The Frame came to her feet, blazing mad, one strand of hair falling across her face, and Root's gun shifted accurately towards her middle. "That's a lie," she screamed. "That's a horrible lie!"

"It's outrageous," said Pell. He was white and trembling. "I'll sue you!"

I went over to the desk and put my knuckles on it and looked them over. "Root ought to knock you off right now, you murderous bunch of bastards! But maybe it'll be better to let the people handle you. I've got a lot of faith in the people, when they get mad. They're violent. They'll tear you to shreds. Particularly you—" I looked at The Frame. "The women will handle you!"

"You don't really believe—" The Frame began. There was astonishment and fear in her voice. It made me feel good.

"Believe! I know. Wait until they find out! Wait until they find out that the same bunch of fiends who blew up Mississippi, and sterilized all the men, also kidnapped Mr. Adam. In twenty-four hours there won't be enough of you left to be worth burying!"

Homer managed to struggle to his feet. His face was so white that I could see freckles where I had never seen freckles before. "Kathy," he said. "Kathy, that wasn't the plan, was it? It wasn't that. Tell me it wasn't anything like that. Is that why you have that apparatus upstairs?"

She looked at him, across the heads of her father and Pell, and said, gravely and with all anger gone from her, "No, Homer, it wasn't anything like that. Those machines are for elementary experimentation to test the effect of radio-active rays on the male germ. We were going to take the utmost precautions not to harm you."

Professor Ruppe spoke for the first time. He was, except for Root, the calmest of us all. "Kitty," he said, "I can see that what we have done, and what we hoped to do, would be hopelessly misunderstood. Hadn't you better tell it all?"

"I think that's best," said Pflaum. "I don't want any mobs tearing my arms out by the roots, or hanging me to a flagpole in front of the Capitol."

"Yes," I agreed. "It would be nice to know what's really going on."

"Do you agree, Dr. Pell?" The Frame asked.

"What is this, a round table discussion?" Root asked. "If you've got anything to say you'd better say it quick."

"I agree," Pell said. His head lolled forward on his chest, as if his neck could no longer support it.

The Frame brushed the hair from her face. "In the first place," she began, "I feel we ought to apologize to Homer. It is true that I persuaded him to leave N.R.P., well, under false pretenses. But it was the only thing we could think of, if we were to act in time. We were just getting around to explaining to Homer when you came in." She regarded Homer directly, even brazenly, I thought, and said, "When I'm finished, I'm not sure that Homer won't agree with our point of view."

"Just forget the propaganda," I said, "and start putting one plain word after another."

"Very well, Steve, don't be so damn overbearing! Here's the way it is, as we see it. The aftereffects of the Mississippi explosion were terrible, certainly, and yet civilization was presented with its one great opportunity to really begin over again—to really create a splendid and decent world, peopled entirely by splendid and decent humans."

"All of them with their master's degree in science," I suggested.

"If you don't shut up," she said, "I shan't continue."

"Go ahead. So what happened?"

"You ought to know. You were in the middle of it, and partly responsible. It was bad enough that the government gave Homer to the N.R.P., and approved A.I., instead of turning him over to the National Research Council. But to make matters worse, no provision whatsoever was made for the scientific selection of future mothers. Here we were presented with this magnificent opportunity, and what do we do? A blindfolded man reaches into a goldfish bowl, and the future of the race is decided literally by blind chance. Not only that, but consider some of the creatures the Congress picked to possess a number in that bowl. When mated to Homer, what else could they produce but red-headed monsters?"

"Oh, I see," I said with what I hoped was sarcasm. "So you people decided to snatch Homer, and present him with a restricted and exclusive clientele. Perhaps you were going to farm him out among your brain-heavy friends, and populate the world with a lot of fine specimens like Dr. Pell here."

The Frame actually looked shocked. "Oh, no!" she protested. "We weren't going to use Homer at all! Not for direct conception. Why, I think Homer himself would be the first to agree that it is a mistake for him to father children—any children at all—if we are to produce a superior race for posterity."

"Gosh, Kathy," Homer said, "I never thought you felt that way about me. I know I'm not very pretty, and I wasn't a Quiz Kid, but I don't think you've got any right to say I'm unfit to have children."

"Don't you?" The Frame asked, the corners of her mouth touched with humor. She paused, and added: "Homer, I think you're sweet, and I'm really very fond of you. Intellectually, I think you'd do, but physically—"

"Don't pay any attention to her, Homer," I advised him, watching the impact of her words crush him back into his chair. "This theory of a superior race isn't original at all. Hitler had one too. The only difference is that Hitler had his master race all set up, and she wants to start hers from scratch."

"I wouldn't put it that way," said Professor Ruppe. "I think most intelligent men will acknowledge the soundness of our theories."

I noticed that Tex Root's gun was no longer in his hand. It had vanished as miraculously as it had appeared. "This is all very interesting," Root said, "but if you weren't going to use Adam, what or who were you going to use?"

"We were going to use Adam, but not for A.I., or any other kind of conception," The Frame explained. "Homer is a source of priceless experimental matériel—the only source. We simply intended to borrow Homer for a few days, for experimental purposes. We had reached a stage in our experiments where it was absolutely necessary to have Homer for a few days. And we knew that once A.I. started we'd never again, perhaps, have a chance to use him. If we were able to use Homer for a short time we felt that we'd find a way—oh, it might take years—but eventually we'd find a way to restore the fertility of other men. Then, we could choose the best males and females, and in a few generations we'd have enough perfect humans so that paired with the inevitably poor stock produced by A.I., matters would not be hopeless."

"And Homer—what were you going to do with him?" I asked.

"We hadn't thought much about that. You see, after his services were no longer necessary, we could proceed with our work, which

is the only important thing. I suppose we would have simply told
Homer to walk home."

"And the repercussions from such action?"

Kathy shrugged. "After he returned, everyone would have been
relieved, and it would be forgotten. Anyway, most people would believe it was simply a clandestine affair. Wouldn't they, Steve?"

I think I whistled. "Kathy," I said, "you're a wicked, ruthless woman."

"All women are ruthless," she replied, "when they're really after
something. And as for being wicked—the N.R.P. is wicked, but
what we are attempting is, I feel, simply acting as instruments of
the will of God."

Her eyes were shining, as I had seen them before. I asked Root,
"How about them, Tex? What are you going to do with them?"

Root considered this, carefully appraising The Frame, and her
father, and Pell, and Canby. He was measuring them, I knew, for
signs of deceit and trickery, as an experienced tailor measures with
his eyes a length of cloth. "I don't see how I can hold them for kidnaping," he said. "Anyway, it sounds more like an intramural scrap
within the government than anything else. That is, unless Adam
wants to bring charges against them. Even then, I don't see what
charges he can bring, except maybe breach of promise."

"Oh, no. No charges," said Homer. "All I want to do is get out of
here."

He was desperate with shame. "Well," I told The Frame, "you
may be stacked, and you're certainly clever, but when it comes to the
snatch racket you're a dope." I suppose I said it more in revenge for
the hurt she had inflicted on Homer than anything else.

"This isn't over," she said quietly, "not yet."

I looked at my watch, and was amazed to find it wasn't yet
twelve. It seemed that we had been away from the hotel for a day or
two. I thought of Mary Ellen, and what news of this might do to her.
"Root," I said, "I think we'd better keep this whole thing as quiet as
possible, don't you?"

"That's okay with me," Root said.

"Please," said Pell. "Please, no publicity. It is bad enough as it is. I do feel, now, that perhaps we went too far. But we were only doing what we thought was the sole right thing to do."

"Well, please don't try it any more," I warned him, "because from now on if anything happens to Adam something is going to happen to you too. Something fatal."

Kathy was smiling again, in a way that wasn't funny. "I'm sure everything will work out all right. I'm quite sure, now. Please go home, because you bore me."

Outside the night air was cool and clean. "Smells good, doesn't it, Homer?" I said.

He didn't answer. "I'm not sore at you, Homer. I'm not blaming you a bit. It wasn't your fault."

We got into Root's sedan, Homer and I in the back. He didn't say anything. I felt he should say something. "Homer," I said, "there's been no damage. Things have just been delayed for a day."

He put his head in his hands and pulled at his hair. "Oh, what a fool I was," he said, the words forcing their way out of him. "What a fool, fool, fool!"

"Don't feel that way Homer. You're not the first guy who has been taken by a scheming bitch. It happens to millions, every year. Lots of them smarter than you. Usually, they're after money, or want to get their names in the Social Register, or run a business from behind the scenes. With you, there was a different motive, but in every other way it was exactly the same. Just tell yourself, 'I've been taken,' and then forget about it."

He didn't answer. He kept his face buried in his hands.

Root parked the car in the hotel driveway and we all got out and Homer walked to the elevator silent and stiff-legged as if he were going to a place of execution.

Marge was waiting for us at the door. "Just like Cinderella, on the stroke of twelve!" she said. "Homer, I'm so glad to see you back."

He walked past her without speaking, and she looked at his face and didn't say anything more. He walked to his bedroom, and lunged inside and shut the door behind him.

"What's wrong with him?" she asked. "What happened? Should I bring him a drink, or anything?"

"We'd better leave him alone," I said. "He's had a harrowing experience." Root went to the telephone, and called his office, and began talking, and while he was on the phone I told Marge what had happened.

When Root was finished with the phone I took it. I called Gableman, at his home, and told him Homer was back. "I'm very glad to hear it," he said, with about as much interest as if he had just heard that his second cousin, in Des Moines, had been elected secretary of the Kiwanis. "But I'm through, Steve. I've taken that job in Interior, and I think if you are smart you will remove yourself from N.R.P. and go back to the AP. If I know anything about the government at all, I know that it is neither smart nor healthy to stay with N.R.P. Good night, Steve."

I called Klutz. He said he was delighted, but his voice sounded shaky. He said he hoped there wouldn't be any publicity, and I assured him there wouldn't be any. He said that was fine, and he would visit Mr. Pumphrey in the hospital first thing in the morning and tell him the good news, and he was sure this would speed Mr. Pumphrey's recovery.

I called Danny Williams. He said he'd pass the word along to the President right away. He asked me what had happened, and I told him I didn't think I could describe it adequately over the telephone, but that anyway Homer was back, and seemed undamaged.

When I was finished Root was putting on his topcoat, and nibbling at the edge of a cracker. "Well, good night," he said. "If anything more happens don't call me. Call somebody else—anybody. This business is too much for me."

"Are you completely satisfied," I said, "that they weren't really going to knock him off?"

"No," he admitted, "not completely."

"I'm not either," I told him. "I still think that Pell is a villain."

Tex Root shook his head. "Spies, I can catch," he said. "Kidnaping for ransom is a cinch. Murder and bond thefts and embezzlement are normal activities. But this is different. This, I don't like. I can't tell who is a criminal, and who isn't, and I can't tell right from wrong. For all I know this Kathy Riddell—and she is a remarkable woman, isn't she?—well, she may be perfectly right. All my life I'll wonder whether what I've done tonight didn't put the world back ten thousand years. Good night, Steve. Good night, Marge. Pleasant dreams."

"Wait a minute," I said. "What do you think I ought to do?"

"If I were you," he said, before he closed the outer door, "I would retreat to Little America."

I went into Homer's room. He was undressed, and in bed, the pillow pulled over his head so I could not tell whether or not he was asleep, and his feet hanging nakedly over the bed's end. As I put out his light I told myself that we really should get a special extra long bed for Homer.

Out in the living room Marge was folding up dresses. "What are you doing?" I asked.

"Packing," she said.

CHAPTER 13

I didn't sleep late the next morning. A sense of urgency ploughed me out of bed before Marge was awake. I tiptoed into Homer's room, and gently opened the door. He was asleep, and snoring, but his bed looked as if it had been occupied by a threshing machine. I ran up coffee and toast in the kitchenette, and then caught Arthur Godfrey's first news. "Well," he said cheerily, "in case you celebrated A.I. Day yesterday you can have all the fun all over again, because it is going to be today. The White House announced early this morning that everything will go ahead according to schedule, but it will be twenty-four hours late."

Homer came into the kitchenette. He was wearing a striped dressing gown, ludicrously short, and when he leaned against the refrigerator somehow he looked like a beach umbrella that has been stacked for the season. "Can I have some coffee?" he said.

"Certainly, Homer." I gave him plenty of sugar and cream. "Well, feel better today?" I asked.

"Oh, I feel all right, Steve, but I don't think you're going to feel very well."

"Why not?"

"In case you think this is A.I. Day, you had better think again," Homer said quietly. "At least so far as I am concerned. What I said yesterday about resigning goes double. I'm through."

"Now, Homer—"

"Sorry, Steve. It's all over."

"Now, Homer, why get those notions in your head? You know as well as I do that there isn't any way out of it. Look at the trouble you got into yesterday when you went off half-cocked. Why make it more difficult for yourself."

"I've thought it all out, Steve. It isn't going to be difficult for me. But from now on it is going to be damn difficult for women."

I didn't like the way he was talking. He was too sure of himself. "For women?" I said.

"Yes. To hell with them. To hell with them all."

"Why, Homer, you of all people shouldn't be talking like that."

Homer drank his coffee, unconcerned, and refilled his cup. "Why not?"

"Because you're fated to have so much to do with them."

"Oh, no I'm not. From now on I'm going to have no more to do with them than is absolutely necessary—excepting Mary Ellen and little Eleanor—of course."

"But won't that still be quite a lot?"

"No. You see, I've figured it all out. If I don't want to go through with A.I. there isn't any way you can force me, now is there?"

Somehow, this was a possibility I had never considered. I said, "No, I suppose there isn't, but—"

"Well, I'm not going through with it. If you take me to the laboratories today, it will be because you are dragging me there by the heels, and if you get me there I can assure you that nothing will happen, except perhaps some surgical equipment and instruments will get broken up."

"Oh, Homer!" I said, not without admiration.

"Will they suffer!" he gloated. "Will they scream!"

Marge came in, sleepy and a little surprised to find us there, and said, "What a cozy little kaffeeklatsch. Can I join you?"

"Yes, but you'll wish you hadn't," I told her. "Homer has decided not to go on. He has said to hell with it all, particularly women."

"Well, can you blame him?" Marge said, with her delightful inconsistency. "If I were Homer I wouldn't have anything to do with women either."

Homer leaned over, in something resembling a bow. "In my list of exceptions to what I just said, I will include Marge."

"You see, Homer," I argued, "most women are pretty decent, like Marge. You just had the misfortune to encounter a particularly wicked and talented wench."

"To hell with them all," Homer said. "I don't think there is any use in discussing the subject further. I want to go back to Tarry-town."

"Now, Homer," I told him, "please don't get me in any more trouble. It's true I can't force you to go through with A.I., but on the other hand I cannot take the responsibility of letting you return to Tarrytown. If anything is done, it will have to be done officially. All I can do is report your decision to N.R.P., and the White House."

"Okay, Steve," he agreed calmly. "Let's have some more coffee."

I could hear the phone ringing in the living room, and Jane answered, and called for me, and said it was Mr. Klutz. I picked it up, and said "Good morning, Percy."

"Good morning, indeed," said Klutz. "I just reached the office, and the Planning Board is meeting in a few moments, and I'd like to report to them on Mr. Adam. How does he feel this morning?"

"He feels fine. Never saw him look better."

"Ah, that's splendid. Poor Mr. Pumphrey was so cheered when

I told him Adam had returned. I think that within a few days he'll have completely recovered."

"I don't," I said.

"You what?"

"I don't think Mr. Pumphrey will quickly recover, if news of Adam has anything to do with it, because you see, Percy, Homer Adam has decided not to go through with A.I."

I could hear Klutz gasp. "Him!" he shouted. "What right has he to decide such a thing? That's a matter for the Inter-Departmental Committee, and the Congress, and the Planning Board! He's got nothing to do with it!"

"Oh, I'm afraid he has," I said.

"Absurd!"

"Well, if you think it is absurd," I suggested, "take him down to the laboratories today and try to make him do something he doesn't want to do."

Homer was standing at my elbow, listening. He was smiling. "Steve," he said, "you certainly have caught on to the idea."

On the other end of the line Klutz was babbling, but he wasn't making any sense. Finally he said, "I'll present the matter to the Planning Board, and I'll let you know their decision."

"What can they decide?"

"Ah, what's that? What can the Planning Board decide? Well, they can turn the whole business over to the Inter-Departmental Committee, and then if necessary it can follow the proper channel to the attention of the President."

"And the President, what can he do about it?"

"Why, he can—now look, Mr. Smith, you'd better do something about this. You're responsible for him, you know."

"Sorry, there's not a thing I can do."

Klutz didn't say anything for so long a time I thought the line was dead, but finally he managed to speak. "I believe," he said, "I will take my annual leave. I haven't taken my annual leave for several years, and I have accumulated eighty-one days. I am afraid this is too much for me, and I need a rest. But first I will inform the Planning Board, and then I am going to take my annual leave. Goodbye, Mr. Smith."

Homer sprawled in a chair, grinning. "Well," he said, "how did the little son-of-a-bitch take it?"

I think all of us jumped, because Homer rarely, if ever, used any expressions more powerful than hell or damn. I knew then that he was a changed man. He had grown up. "He's going on leave, which means that he's running away," I said, and then I added, "Homer, just between you and me and Marge and Jane, I don't blame you a bit, and whatever you do, I'm for you."

"I am too," said Jane. "Homer, I don't know whether you're doing the right thing, or the wrong thing, but at least you are doing it yourself, and for you I think that's important."

"I do too," said Marge. "You know how I feel about having babies. But Homer, you do whatever you think best. Don't you let Steve shove you around any more."

"Me?" I said. "I'm not going to shove him around. But I am going to take him to the White House, and let him tell Danny Williams, or maybe the President, about it. I don't want this on my head."

"Sure. Glad to," said Homer. "Let's dress and go."

So we dressed, and I called Danny Williams, and told him it was vital, or more so, and he said the President could squeeze Homer in at 11:15, between the new Minister from Iraq, and the Joint Chiefs of Staff, who at that moment were disturbed by the prospect that the war being officially declared over, a good many officers would be forced to revert to their permanent rank. I told Danny Williams what Homer had decided, and he told me not to worry, because the Boss would handle it. I said I hoped so. As I look at it now, I don't know whether I hoped so or not.

The White House ritual is precise and exact. It is a super assembly line designed to turn out the maximum number of interviews with the President in the minimum time. I put Homer into one end of the assembly line, and then for fifteen minutes I chatted with Danny Williams—in the office that Steve Early used to inhabit— until he came out. When he came out he was still grinning. I knew that he had won, and I felt sort of proud of him, but I also believed the world had ended.

Danny Williams sensed it too. As he walked us to our car he said, "Steve, I'll call you later."

It wasn't much later, because Homer had laid an explosive with a short fuse on the President's desk. When we got back to the hotel Jane said, "You're to call the White House immediately."

So I called Danny Williams, and he had lost his usual calm and was sputtering like an eight-cylinder engine trying to run on kerosene. "Look, Steve," he said, "this is catastrophic. Do you know what Adam told the Boss?"

"Sure I know," I said. "He told him he wasn't going through with it. He said he was resigning."

"Oh, that isn't all," Danny Williams said. "He told the President—I don't think I'd better tell you what he told the President, not over the phone."

"Was it something about women?" I suggested.

"It certainly was something about women. I must say the Boss is shocked. He thinks Adam is a little tetched, and he is gravely concerned about allowing A.I. to continue, even if we bring Adam around. As a matter of fact he has decided to postpone A.I. indefinitely, and turn Adam over to the National Research Council. They claim they need him."

"Oh, boy! Oh, boy, oh boy!"

"What's the matter?"

"Well, if you think Adam is allergic to women, wait until he finds out he's going to be handed over to the scientists."

Danny began to sputter again. "Up here in the White House,"

he said, "we're getting damn sick and tired of Adam's temperament. We're for the rights of individual citizens, and the Constitution, and all that, but the rights of the nation transcend the rights of the citizen, on occasion, and believe me this is the occasion."

"I'm sure Adam would agree with that, in theory, but when you practice it on him he doesn't like it, and he's liking it less every minute. His is a very special case."

"Not any more it isn't. From now on the status of Adam is that of a valuable experimental animal. Now that sounds crude and harsh, I know, but that's the way it has to be. The Army will have charge of his feeding and his welfare, and if necessary, they can hold him just exactly as a political prisoner would be held. And the N.R.C. can perform whatever experiments they see fit. That's final. The executive order will be out today."

"So be it," I said. "For my part, I will be delighted to get out of this town—this madhouse in marble. I think if I stayed one more day they'd have me in St. Elizabeth's. However, I don't think you can change a man's feelings or his character by executive order, and I am afraid there is going to be trouble, or more trouble."

"That's a chance we have to take," Danny said. "And I want to tell you that we appreciate your help. The President will send you a letter."

"I'd frame it," I told him, "for my grandchildren, except that I'm not going to have any grandchildren. And I don't like to be pessimistic, but I don't think you are either, Danny."

Homer and Marge and Jane were tilting early highballs in the kitchenette. Marge and Jane were trying to persuade Homer to describe the White House conference, and Homer was naturally somewhat reticent, if not downright evasive. "Well," I told them, "I've been fired, but Homer, you've got a new job."

"I was hoping he'd fire me too," said Homer. "I certainly tried to get fired."

"Oh, no, Homer, you're the indispensable man."

"What's the new job?" he asked.

I hesitated. I wanted to present Homer's new job in the best possible light, simply because I didn't want him blowing up on my hands. "In the first place," I said, "you don't have to worry about A.I. any more. A.I. is finished, and Fay Sumner Knott becomes Would-be A.I. Mother Number One."

"Now we're getting somewhere," Homer said.

"From now on," I continued, "you will work for the National Research Council."

"You mean Pell and his gang?"

"Well, I believe Dr. Pell is a director of N.R.C."

"You can just call the White House about my new job," Homer said firmly. "Tell them I quit."

"It isn't that simple, Homer. You can't quit. As I said, you're the indispensable man."

"What do you mean, I can't quit?"

"I mean—well, I might as well tell you exactly what it is—you are practically the same as under house arrest. You have lost your rights. You are like one hundred and sixty pounds of U-235."

I had expected Homer to blow up, but he appeared completely cool, and an elfin grin lit his face up again. "They'll regret it," he said.

"Now, Homer, there isn't any use trying to be belligerent, because the Army has been placed in charge of you."

"If they want another Pearl Harbor," Homer said, "that's what they're going to get."

He finished his drink, and poured himself another. A queer metamorphosis had taken place in Homer Adam, working from the inside out. His timidity was gone, and as he stood there, drink in hand, his tousled hair an arrogant flame, he looked to me like some of those wild Irishmen you will find in Cherry Hill bars, ready to stack all the other customers in a corner just for the hell of it.

By the time General Kipp, commanding Eastern Defense Command, Zone of the Interior, arrived with Colonel Phelps-Smythe, Homer was a little tight around the edges. Their entrance was rather awkward, as if it hadn't been properly rehearsed. They were accompanied by second lieutenants, complete with sidearms, and a photographer.

General Kipp, perspiring and unhappy, grasped Homer's hand, and shook it, and the photographer unloosed a bulb. "My dear Mr. Adam," Kipp said woodenly, as if he were making a radio speech and had difficulty reading the script, "I hope you are well."

"Take the glass out of his hand," said Phelps-Smythe. A second lieutenant took the glass out of Homer's hand, and they started again. "My dear Mr. Adam," the general repeated, "I hope you are well."

"Give me back my drink," said Homer.

"Give him back his drink," the general ordered the second lieutenant.

The photographer took another shot, and the second lieutenant gave the drink back to Homer.

"How are things?" the general inquired.

"Things are very drunk out today," Homer said.

"What's that?" said Phelps-Smythe. "What was that you said, Adam?"

"You can take the National Research Council, plus three large cyclotrons, and you can—" I don't think there is any use repeating what Homer told Phelps-Smythe, because such things are said every day. But Homer Adam's saying them was new. So I listened.

Phelps-Smythe puffed out like a turkey gobbler trying to impress his hens with his bravery. "Adam," he said, "we are through with all this damn foolishness. From now on, Adam, you'll take orders! By God, you will!"

"He will indeed!" General Kipp agreed.

"No," said Adam, "I won't."

Phelps-Smythe felt around in his pockets and came up with a mimeographed sheet of paper, legal size. He put his heels together and read from it as if it were the Articles of War. "This," he began, "is the directive prepared by the War Department and signed by the President:

SUBJECT: HOMER ADAM.

1. Homer Adam, civilian, is hereby declared Class AAA Strategic Material vital to the defense of the United States.
2. The Department of War will be responsible for the maintenance and security of this property.
3. Homer Adam, civilian, will at all times be subservient to, and conduct himself according to whatever rules and regulations shall be promulgated by the Chief of Staff, or Adjutant General, to carry out the purpose of Paragraphs 1 and 2.
4. The National Research Council shall have the opportunity to use said Homer Adam for purposes of research upon the approval of the Joint Chiefs of Staff, but this in no way shall interfere with Paragraph 2."

Phelps-Smythe folded his directive, and tucked it into a hip pocket. "There," he said, "now you see."

"Now I see what?" said Homer.

"Now you see where things stand. I guess that directive is pretty air tight, isn't it, General?"

"I'll say it is," said General Kipp. "That doesn't leave any doubt about who's in control. The N.R.C. can't do a damn thing until they've got approval from the Joint Chiefs."

Adam was thinking. "Does that mean," he asked, "that nothing is going to happen?"

"Certainly not!" Phelps-Smythe said. "That only means that before the N.R.C. can do anything it has to have the approval of the Joint Chiefs of Staff, which means Army, Navy, and Air. And of course before the Joint Chiefs approve anything it will require a staff study from each branch of the service, and proposals will have to be made by the experts in each branch, and it probably will require special surveys to find the effect on the existing situation. Furthermore, public opinion must be considered. That's why we have a Public Relations Branch, and in addition, the international situation cannot be overlooked. And of course the whole thing will have to be co-ordinated with the War Plans Division. Isn't that so, General?"

"That is it, precisely," said General Kipp.

"Why can't I take a little vacation?" Homer asked.

"Vacation!" shouted Phelps-Smythe. "Vacation! Now let me tell you, young man, this foolishness is all over. From now on your life is strictly business. Right at the first, I think we'll send you to one of the O.C. camps and give you a little basic training. Do you good. Just what you need. Knock this cockiness out of you."

"I won't do it," said Homer.

"You won't do it!" exploded Phelps-Smythe. "From now on you haven't got anything to say about what you'll do or won't do."

"Oh, yes I have," said Homer. "If you keep on being nasty, I won't eat."

Phelps-Smythe started to say something, but General Kipp checked him and told Homer, "Now we don't want any trouble, Adam. We're only doing our duty as soldiers, you know. Come on, let's get going."

So they took Homer away. Just as he left, Phelps-Smythe turned to me and said, "Remember, Smith—you and that Red secretary of yours—all this is Top Secret."

Marge made a face at him, but I don't think he noticed it.

We caught the Congressional back to New York. It didn't take us long to get out of the hotel, because Marge had done most of the packing the night before. This I laid to intuition, but she denied it, and said it was only common sense. She claimed that I was addled, perhaps by strain, and wasn't able to see things with the proper perspective. She said that immediately after a man is kicked in the teeth by a woman, a great clarity creeps into his brain, and that this clarity persists until scar tissue—in the shape of another woman—grows over his memory.

Just before we got on the train I bought a late edition of an evening paper. The headline said: "ADAM BALKS; A.I. OUT!" and under this was another headline, which read: "Army Takes Over; President for N.R.C." There was a front page editorial, entitled, "No Cause for Alarm."

CHAPTER 14

So we settled down in the brownstone house on West Tenth Street, first floor; the bed known as Smith Field, and resumed our normal mode of living. I found myself doing eight hours of rewrite a day, and liking it. It was like occupational therapy. I wrote about the opening of the state trout season, and I covered the Easter Parade on Fifth Avenue, and I wrote a piece about the selection of the country's ten best-dressed men.

I rewrote our cables from Delhi and Chungking about the famine, but of course that could hardly be considered news, because it was a running story, the same day after day. I wrote about the over-production of pigs, and the shortage of meat; the bumper wheat crop, and the possible rationing of bread; the need for subsidies for the Southern cotton farmers, and the black market in textiles; our record employment, and our record poverty. In God's Country everything was normal, and for a considerable space of time nothing disturbed our American Way of Life.

I kept an eager eye open for dispatches from Washington about

Mr. Adam. In the AP report, you could always find the slug, "Adam."
Even when there was no news of Homer, I knew that somebody in
the AP Bureau in Washington had to sit down and write a piece
about him, and his progress, every night, and around noon some
reporter sat himself before a typewriter, confronted by a slug saying,
"New lead Adam."

So I kept watching Adam, just as a released suspect in a murder
keeps alert for news of the crime. Mostly, the Adam stories were
wooden and almost newsless. The N.R.C. was confident that, now it
had been placed in charge of Adam, science would solve the riddle of
what had happened to the world post-Mississippi. The N.R.C. had
enlisted all the top scientists of the country in the scientific battle
for re-fertilization. The N.R.C. requested more funds from the President, and claimed it must expand to meet the crisis.

Having once been stricken with the disease, I found the sym-
toms familiar. I was not overly surprised when one day I read, in
a single paragraph on page twenty-two of the *World-Telegram*, that
Percy Klutz, formerly of N.R.P., had joined N.R.C. as administrative assistant. Nor was I surprised when I read that Nate Gableman,
an experienced public relations expert, had been loaned to N.R.C.
by the Department of the Interior, where he had just arrived from
N.R.P. Prior to that, Gableman had held a number of government
positions. About a half dozen of them were listed.

However, that was all S.O.P. What was truly puzzling were some
of the stories out of the War Department. There was a little squib
that said the War Department was sending Homer Adam to Camp
Blanding, in Florida, to absorb sunshine and recreation, because his
duties in Washington had been so arduous. There were stories about
meetings of the Joint Chiefs, at which a number of things were discussed, including Arctic maneuvers, and Mr. Adam. The War Department sometimes said its Arctic maneuvers were not directed at
any specific power, but really at the elements, but it never explained
about about Mr. Adam. Finally, there were stories about the difficul-

ties of using Mr. Adam, and hints that Adam wasn't really essential, at all. He could be useful, it was admitted, but the N.R.C. didn't regard him as absolutely essential.

One day Marge and I went to a double-header between the Yanks and the Nats. We were propped up on our pillows in Smith Field, watching the remnants of the immortal Yankees make fools of themselves around second base, and I was telling Marge about Ruth and Gehrig and Dickey, and without warning my favorite sports announcer, Malcolm Parkinson, poked his ruddy face into our bedroom, and said, inspecting a sheet of yellow teletype paper:

"Well, folks, I'm sorry to have to interrupt this ball game, but we've just received an important news flash. But before I read this flash I want to tell you that for calm nerves—nerves able to withstand the shock of modern living—smoke . . ." And he went on, and on. Finally he finished his commercial, and said, "And here is that flash, folks. Homer Adam ruined! Yes, sir, a flash from Washington tells us that Homer Adam has been ruined. That is all for now, but as we receive additional details we'll give them to you, so you might as well keep tuned to this exciting ball game, with the Yanks gamely fighting against a driving Washington team which at this moment has a six run lead. And the next batter for the Nats it . . ."

I switched him off, and his face faded off the screen, looking a bit disturbed. "I knew it!" I said. "I knew it would happen."

"You knew what?" Marge asked.

"I knew that they'd sterilize Homer!"

"How do you know he was sterilized? All they said was that he was ruined."

"How else could he be ruined?"

"Oh!" Marge said. "Isn't that awful!"

I turned on our bedside radio. It was beside itself. It rattled as if men from Mars had appeared, and it wished to duck under the sheets. It said that the War Department had informed the President that the National Research Council had sterilized Mr. Adam. It said this had happened several weeks ago. It said that the announcement was withheld until it was utterly certain that Mr. Adam had been sterilized. It said that the National Research Council announced it was a complete accident. The War Department agreed with the N.R.C. that it was a complete accident, and the President agreed with the War Department. Nobody was to blame.

Marge stared at the radio as if it were foul and repugnant and untouchable. "There it goes," she whispered.

"There goes what?"

"Everything. Just everything. That pitiful little man!"

"He's not pitiful," I said, simply for something to say.

"He is. He is, too, pitiful. When I think what's happened to him it makes me feel unclean, as if I'd seen a murder, and hadn't done anything to stop it."

"We all did our best," I said.

"Did we?" she asked, not of me, but of herself. "Did we really?"

I felt a little wave of anger and resentment ripple over me, like the first chill that heralds the onset of fever. I wasn't exactly sure at whom I was angry, but somebody had hurt and damaged my wife, and I wanted to strike back. I wondered who had sterilized Adam, and how, and why. Somehow, the radio didn't go into that part of it. The radio contented itself with announcing that Homer Adam had been ruined, and then erudite commentators rushed to the microphones to assure us that the ruination of Adam wasn't necessarily fatal to mankind. Their conjectures were that Adam had already contributed as much as he could to science, and anyway, Russia had never denied possessing the two potent Mongolians. Looking at the whole matter logically, and without undue hysteria, it could be seen that the loss of Adam's services wasn't so important after all. Perhaps the situation in Indo-China was of more immediate importance, and they spoke learnedly of the situation in Indo-China.

Our telephone rang, and it was J.C. Pogey, and he wanted to know whether I'd heard the news, and I said I had, and he said, "I think you'd better handle the local angle on the Adam story?"

"What local angle?" I asked.

He said there were a good many local angles. He reminded me that some of the N.R.C. directors lived in New York, and that they should be interviewed, and Adam himself had returned to Tarrytown, according to the Washington Bureau. The story wasn't by any means cleaned up. As a matter of fact, the details of Adam's sterilization remained a mystery. I said I'd get right on it, and as I shaved and dressed the pattern began to take shape in my mind. The first person I was going to visit was Felix Pell. He might be the last, too.

I tried to remember where I had cached the Browning. It was my one souvenir of the war, a handsomely machined, Belgian-made automatic. I rummaged through the hall closet until I found it, and Marge saw me drop it into my coat pocket. "Stephen! Why are you taking that gun?" she demanded.

I didn't reply.

"Don't be ridiculous. If the police find that gun they'll throw you in jail because of the Sullivan law. Anyway, you can't hit anything with it more than ten feet away."

"What I'm going to shoot," I said, "won't be more than ten feet away."

Marge stared at me, astonished as if I'd just announced I was a bigamist. "Stephen," she said, "are you serious?"

"I am," I said.

"I won't let you go out of the house with that weapon."

I took her by the shoulders. Maybe I was a little rough. I said, "Darling, up to now I have been a mild and civilized man. But now I have a killing to do."

I left before she could say anything more.

I went up to Columbia, and the home of Felix Pell. The maid opened the door a crack, and I could see it was secured by a chain latch. On occasion, I think it is fair to use deception. Mostly I think it is crude and stupid, but once in a while, when the stakes are high enough, it is the only thing to do. "Quickly," I said, "undo that chain and let me in. Before the reporters come. They'll be here in a minute."

She blinked at me, and said, "Dr. Pell told me especially he doesn't want to see reporters." She unhooked the latch and let me in.

"Naturally not," I said.

"I don't think he wants to see anybody," she said. "Who are you?"

"Tell him Mr. Smith is calling," I said, "on a matter of greatest importance." She scuttled upstairs, and I followed her. I followed her into Pell's bedroom, morose with old-fashioned walnut furniture. Pell was propped up in bed, his picturesque head supported by pillows. He glared at me, one eye winking erratically. Since I had last seen him, he had developed a tic.

The maid looked at Pell, and she looked at me, and she saw that we knew each other, and she vanished. "How did you get in here?" he demanded.

The standard defense, in a killing, is that everything either goes black, or it goes red, and in any case the first thing the killer knows is that the other person is dead and he is standing there with a smoking gun in his hand. The verdict, his attorney hopes, will be temporary insanity. It isn't exactly like that. It is simply that things are hazy, and move with annoying slowness. I took the Browning out of my pocket. The hammer caught in the lining, and it seemed a long time before I ripped it loose. I thumbed the safety, and it released with a definite click. A nice, final, decisive sound, that click. "This isn't going to be much satisfaction for anyone except me," I said, "but for me it will be fun."

"You're out of your head," Pell said clinically. "You're unbalanced."

I was going to shoot him through the middle of the chest, just under the chin, where the hem of his old-fashioned nightgown met the pallid flesh. Then I was going to shoot him again, in the same place, to make sure. "So you finished off Homer Adam," I said. "You were very thorough, and very clever. And it was all a deplorable accident! A most deplorable accident!"

"No, it wasn't an accident," Pell said.

"I know it wasn't an accident. You finished off Homer Adam, and everyone else, deliberately, just as I'm going to slam a nine-millimeter slug through you deliberately."

He dropped back against his pillows. "All right," he said, "go ahead." He folded his dried, tallow-yellow hands, one against the other, and repeated, "Go ahead. I am tired. I am very tired and there is nothing more I can do. I don't suppose it matters whether I die quickly, now, or that I live for several months or years. Please when you shoot be sure I am dead, because I do not want to die slowly."

This was not what I had expected him to say. He was saying all the wrong things. "Tell me," I said, "what have you and your buddies got against humanity that made you do it?"

Dr. Pell groaned. "Against humanity? Why, I haven't got anything against humanity," he said. "I have always felt that I'd devoted my life to humanity. I know you won't believe it now, and considering what you know—the limitations of what you know—I can hardly blame you. Now please go ahead and shoot me."

The Browning was beginning to feel heavy in my hand, and I felt rather ridiculous, standing there, threatening this old man. I let it fall to my side. "That doesn't make sense. You admit that Homer Adam wasn't sterilized by accident, and yet you say——"

"He certainly was not sterilized by accident," Dr. Pell said, anger cracking his voice. "He did it himself!"

"Did it himself?"

"Yes, he committed what amounted to sexual suicide."

This was a possibility that I had not considered. But it was so very possible, and so intriguing, that I knew I could not kill Pell until I found out whether it was so. I shoved the gun back into my pocket, knowing immediately that I would never shoot Pell now, and said, "Tell me about it."

"It is all so exasperating, and so confusing, that I don't like to discuss it," Pell said. "I wish you would please go ahead and kill me, because if I am forced to write a paper on this business I shall certainly lose my mind."

"What's so exasperating and confusing?"

Pell saw that there was no chance that I would shoot him, and he said, with resignation, "I suppose I'd better tell you about it, because I don't think you will leave until I do. In the first place, there were the complications. As you know, we only needed Adam for a few days of tests, but I was never able to get my hands on him. I found that all I was doing was attending meetings and conferences. I believe it was a conspiracy."

"That wasn't a conspiracy," I said. "It was just ordinary procedure."

"Obstacles sprouted from the streets," Pell went on. "People sat up nights thinking up reasons why we couldn't begin operations."

"I know what you mean."

"We were patient. Finally all the boards and committees and panels had approved all their plans, and Adam was delivered to the laboratory. He was calm, and in good health. We were very careful, because much of our equipment and apparatus was designed to reproduce the rays and radiations which we believe were unloosed in the Mississippi explosion. The first thing we did was warn Adam not to walk in certain areas, or go near certain machines."

"And?"

"He was very clever. He waited until we were all distracted with something else—I believe it was the official cameraman—and then he sauntered off. By the time we found him he had sterilized himself thoroughly. He's lucky he's not dead."

"Are you sure?"

"Certainly we're sure. We made every conceivable test. It was the most bewildering, exasperating experience I've ever had in my life. Why did he do it?"

I said I didn't know, but I was going to find out. I started to apologize for coming up to shoot Dr. Pell, but when I tried to form the proper words into a sentence it sounded silly, and all I said was that I was sorry things turned out the way they did, and I hoped he would soon be out of bed.

I caught an evening commuters' train for Tarrytown, and then a cab to the gatehouse at Rosemere. The press had left its spoor, a little pile of used flashlight bulbs, on the front steps. I wondered whether Adam had told the truth, as I rang the bell, and decided probably not, because he had probably been carefully briefed on what to say before he left Washington—an accident, a most unfortunate accident.

Homer opened the door. "Steve!" he said, draping a skinny arm around my shoulders. "I was wondering when you'd get here. It's good to see you. Hey, Mary Ellen," he called upstairs. "Steve finally got here."

She said she was changing diapers, and she would be down presently. "Now that we're not working for the government any more," Homer explained, "we had to let Mrs. Brundidge go, except twice a week."

"Well, while we're here alone," I told him, "tell me why you did it?"

Homer sat down suddenly. His cranelike legs were not made to support him in moments of stress. "How did you know about it?" he asked. "I was hoping no one would know. It is a secret. Everybody said it was not only secret, but top secret, because if it got out it would cause so much trouble, and so many people would be accused of negligence. I don't want to get anybody into trouble."

"Don't worry," I said. "You're not getting anybody into trouble. I've just been talking to Dr. Pell. I was about to shoot Dr. Pell, because I thought he had deliberately sterilized you, and then he said you did it yourself."

"I did," Homer admitted.

"But why? Were you getting back at Kathy?"

Homer glanced at the stairs. "Not so loud," he warned. "Mary Ellen doesn't know there was anything really serious between Kathy and me, and if she hears you mention her, she might suspect something."

"All right, I'll be careful," I agreed, amused at the ignorance of the average male.

"No, it wasn't Kathy," he said in a low, hoarse voice.

"The way you talked about women, I thought—well, I thought you were still vengeful."

"Oh, I think I got over that," Homer said. "As you explained, every man gets taken once in his life."

"Perhaps you were simply fed up with the delays," I suggested, remembering Pell's account of his troubles.

"Oh, no. I got used to delays when the N.R.P. had me."

"Then what in hell was it?"

Homer began to knead his tousled mop of hair with his fingers, and I knew he was finding it difficult to answer. "I'll tell you," he said finally. "It was just me."

"Just you?"

"It was just that I wanted to be like everyone else. All my life I have wanted to be like everyone else, and now I am like everyone else, and for the first time I feel completely right. You know a lot about me, Steve. You know I was always different. I was different when I was a little boy, and I was different when I was adolescent, and I was different when I grew up. Now I'm not different any more."

I tried to sort it out in my head. "When did you decide this?" I asked.

"I'm not sure. I don't think you decide things like that all at once. This is the kind of decision that you climb and scratch for, and when you've finally got it then you know it's all yours. I knew I had reached my decision when Dr. Pell took me into the N.R.C. laboratories. I knew, then, that I was either going to be sterile, like everyone else, or I was going to be dead. I don't know what made me decide, right at that moment. Maybe it was the machines."

"The machines? You mean, you knew that the machines gave you your opportunity?"

"No. Not exactly that. But when I saw the machines I hated them. They were so damn smug. There were a lot of big, pot-bellied machines with snouts and arms, and they all looked alive, and smug. They were exactly like the machines in Pflaum's house, and I felt they had been patiently waiting for me. I hated them, and I wanted to put them out of business, and all of a sudden I knew that if I was out of the way the machines would die. That was when I walked into the range of the radiations. I think it was the Gamma rays first."

"Homer," I said, "it sounds perfectly correct and reasonable to me, but I am glad no psychiatrist is listening."

"I'm glad you don't think there's something wrong with me," Homer said. "There isn't anything wrong with me, now. Why, I'm just like everyone else." It was strange, the way he relished the phrase. It was as if he had happily and unexpectedly been elected to a college fraternity, after a semester of loneliness.

"Yes, Homer, you're just like everyone else," I agreed. "Just exactly."

Mary Ellen came down the steps, carrying the Adam offspring. I reflected on what would have happened had Eleanor been a boy, and said something about it, and Homer said, "Thank goodness she was a girl, because if she had been a boy, he would have had to go through the same thing I had to go through when he grew up."

Mary Ellen said she knew she should feel sorry about what had happened to Homer, but she didn't at all, really. She knew this was selfish, but on the other hand she felt certain something would turn up. She asked what had happened to the two Mongolians, and I said that nobody knew. She said that on one of the nights when Mrs. Brundidge was over she and Homer would come to the city, and visit, and I said that was fine, and I was sure Marge would enjoy having them. She said she hoped the government and the press would leave them alone from now on, because it would be difficult enough getting back into their old routine, and I said that in a few weeks everything would quiet down.

Eleanor began to squall, and Mary Ellen said she was hungry, and took her back upstairs, and Homer said he hoped I wouldn't write anything about what had really happened in the N.R.C. laboratories, because it would get him into trouble. I told him that somebody would get hold of the story, sooner or later, but that when they did nobody would believe it, and if I wrote it now nobody would believe it, so I wasn't going to write it.

I called J. C. Pogey, and then I went home. If I expected Marge to be apprehensive about what I'd done to Dr. Pell I was mistaken. She was putting together a ham steak and pineapple slices, and whistling at her work. "Before you come in here," she said, "you put that gun in the closet, and take out the clip, and be sure there's no bullet in the chamber."

"Aren't you going to ask me whether I killed him?" I said.

"I know you didn't."

I realized I hadn't told her where I was going. "Know I didn't kill who?"

"Why, Dr. Pell, of course. Who else would you be wanting to kill? I called him right after you left his house. He said you were headstrong and not too bright, but ordinarily harmless."

I told her about Homer. "That's what I thought," she said, "from the way Dr. Pell talked."

After dinner we retired to Smith Field, and the radio began to bleat about the new catastrophe—but always with optimistic overtones. It fell upon the theme that Homer was not indispensable, and worried that for a time, and then it began to chew the story of the two Mongolians. In the space of a few hours the two Mongolians became supremely important to the American people.

The Secretary of State had been asked about the status of the two Mongolians, and he said he had the greatest confidence in the fair play of the Russian government, our loyal allies, and he was sure the U.S.S.R. would not hoard them. The Secretary of State suggested that hereafter any unsterilized males should be turned over to the United Nations. If I remember his words correctly, he said, "How can we expect the United Nations to become a strong and independent force for the benefit of all mankind unless it possesses access to the resources of all nations?" It was a brilliant thought, and I was surprised that he hadn't thought of it before.

He pointed out what aid the United States had given Russia, during the war, and went all the way back to the Alaska purchase to recall our constant good relations with Russia. The very spirit of Communism, he pointed out, was devoted to the good of all peoples, and he reminded Russia that the two unsterilized Mongols were citizens of the world, as well as of the U.S.S.R.

There was a dispatch from Chungking hinting that the two Mongolians might not be Russian at all, but Chinese, and requesting that the case be put before the Security Council. London immediately announced it would vote along with China.

And then, just before midnight, a dispatch from Moscow said that the Russian government didn't know a thing about unsterilized Mongolians. The story of the two Mongolians, Moscow said, was undoubtedly part of an anti-Communist plot.

An announcer talked about a laxative that was so soothing for those over thirty-five, and I said I thought it was horrible advertising psychology, and Marge asked why, and I said because it automatically eliminated everyone under thirty-five as a prospective customer. Marge said that wasn't the reason I didn't like it. The reason was because I was over thirty-five, and resented it whenever anyone reminded me of it. And I admitted that was another reason

I didn't like it. And Marge said she thought it was good advertising, now that Adam was finished and the two Mongolians were phoney, because eventually everybody would be over thirty-five.

I don't think she liked the idea, because she was still awake, with her head couched in her arm, when I fell asleep.

I suppose everyone turned out his lights at the usual hour that night. Certainly there was no wailing in the streets.

CHAPTER 15

With Adam ruined, the two Mongolians a myth, the N.R.C. baffled and helpless, and the N.R.P. on the verge of liquidation, the situation was black as a British communiqué the day before Dunkirk. Yet the customs and habits of man kept him revolving in his orbit as inexorably as planets are bound to the sun. The world would not die in agony and convulsions. It would simply expire of old age.

The most popular slogan of the day was "Take it easy," and *Life Begins at Forty* again went to the top of the list of best sellers. The only people who were extremely sensitive to the passing of each childless day were women approaching an age where they would no longer be able to bear children. They formed associations, and demanded that Congress and the Administration do something, but there was nothing to do.

Everyone acquired a little bit of the philosophy of J.C. Pogey, and Pogey himself said mankind was behaving exactly as he had expected. "It is this way," he explained. "If the threat of destruction couldn't jolt us out of our rut—and that threat was apparent long before Mississippi—then the fact of destruction can't be expected to change us much either."

Everything rocked along as usual. The Miami Chamber of Commerce announced that it was planning its biggest season, and that next winter, for certain, Miami would not be overrun with gangsters and racketeers. The airlines started five-day excursions to Paris and Cairo. There was an abundance of nylon stockings, but it became unfashionable to wear them. The housing crisis miraculously passed. Everything was normal—except in my own home.

In my own home the situation suddenly and violently departed from normal. It was Marge. Her entire disposition and character changed, and for the worse.

At first I put it down to delayed shock from the catastrophe that had overtaken Homer. Marge had been more than fond of Homer. Like so many weak men with stronger women, he apparently had appealed to all her protective instincts. In addition, she really had had a good deal of faith in A.I., probably acquired from talking to Maria Ostenheimer. Yet she had accepted the sterilization of Homer Adam without undue emotion.

Now she grew irritable, and touchy, and I blamed it on delayed shock. She was gradually realizing, I believed at first, that Homer's suicidal disaster had doomed her to a barren marriage.

The habit and pattern and tradition of our life together—the small things that two people do together that make them one—were blemished or vanished entirely. These are very small things indeed, but of surpassing importance. There are the private jokes; and the ritual of who wakes first, and puts on the coffee; and who gets what part of the Sunday papers; and my growls because she uses my razor.

The business of the razor ordinarily used to go like this: When I started shaving I would discover that my razor had had it. I would curse and say that there were a few things a man could have in private, and one of them was a razor, and that if she wanted to shave her legs she could easily run over to the drug store on the Avenue of the Americas and buy a razor all her own. And she would say she had bought countless razors, but hers were always dull, and mine was always sharp. And I would say that was because I put fresh blades in mine, and she would say that was part of a man's duty, and I would say I was going to cure her entirely, and take up electric shaving.

And there, ordinarily, was where it ended. But one day in June I was covering an exhibition of electric gadgets and a manufacturer presented all the reporters with electric razors.

The next morning I was running it over my chin when Marge saw me and immediately burst into tears. "You horrid man," she said. "You don't love me any more."

"I don't what?"

"You don't love me any more. For years you've tortured me with threats about buying an electric razor, and now you have gone and done it, simply to show your contempt for me."

I looked at her, and saw she actually was crying. An absurd and maudlin scene developed, at the end of which I threw my electric razor into the trash barrel.

Then there was the matter of getting up nights. Ordinarily Marge sleeps as if she had been hit on the head, until morning, but she began to develop a habit of waking up, at four or five, and then waking me up. "I want a bag of peanuts," she would say, nudging me or kicking me from the other side of Smith Field. Sometimes she would wake up and say she wasn't sure the front door was locked, or would I please get up and bring her a raw egg.

It was all inexplicable, and most unlike her.

The worst of it was her newly acquired jealousy and suspicion. Marge had never been jealous. For one thing, it is silly and futile for a newspaperman's wife to be jealous, just as it is silly and futile for a doctor's wife to be jealous. The uncertain hours and nature of his job provide a newspaperman with so many unimpeachable alibis that if a wife suspects him she will just run herself crazy, and never prove anything. In the second place, Marge simply wasn't jealous. I don't know whether it was confidence in herself, or in me.

Now, each night when I returned from work, she began to drop little fishhooks of questions into her conversation, trying to catch some fancied admission that would prove me unfaithful.

She fished in all the years of our marriage. Incidents that I had long forgotten, and girls of whom I had only the vaguest memory became subjects for hysterical accusations and violent scenes. One evening Marge casually put a magazine aside and said, "That secretary of yours in Washington, Jane Zitter—you saw a lot of her, didn't you?"

"Yes," I said. "She was a big help. Swell girl."

"Stephen, you sort of lived with her, didn't you?"

I saw what was coming. "Now look, Marge," I said. "There wasn't anything between Jane and me except that she was my secretary, and a very good one, too. And if you've got to exercise these silly notions of yours, pick on somebody besides poor Jane."

"Well, you're pretty excited about it, aren't you," she said significantly. "Actually, she did live with you, didn't she?"

I knew I was going to blow up, and I began to pace the floor to relieve the pressure. "Marge, you know as well as I do that sometimes Jane spent the night up in the hotel. In her own bedroom. In her own bed. Nobody with her. Now lay off!"

"You're shouting at me again," she said. "You always shout when you've done something you can't explain. Just because you make a lot of noise doesn't make you less guilty."

I was tired of it. I was tired of Marge and her incessant third degree. But I didn't say anything more. I put on my hat, and went outside, and it was good to be alone. I realized that lately I had been leaving for work earlier than necessary, and returning home as late as possible. I walked over to Fifth Avenue, and then down to Washington Square. I found an empty bench, and sat down and tried to think.

I told myself that I was letting my nerves harass me into a point where I would reach an impasse with Marge, and there would be a divorce, although a divorce since W.S. Day seemed almost as futile as marriage. Then I began to analyze her actions. I tried to place myself in the role of a disinterested spectator. And particularly I began to analyze her spasms of jealousy and suspicion. I told myself that there could be no doubt of it, Marge was ill—mentally ill. She had all the symptoms.

It was quite the most horrible and dismaying conclusion I ever reached. I had never realized, before, that insanity in one close to you is far worse than physical illness, for when a person's mind goes they are completely gone from you, as in death, and yet their body remains. Of course I had to be certain, and once I was certain I must see that she got the very best neurotherapy. I told myself that it probably wasn't incurable. I would ask Maria Ostenheimer and Tommy Thompson over the next night and, without alarming Marge, they could tell whether it was so.

Before I returned home I stopped at a drug store, and called Maria, and told her the whole story, as unemotionally as possible, and from the questions she asked I could see that she was worried, and she promised to come over the next evening for bridge, and she would bring Tommy.

I went to sleep that night trying to remember what I knew of Marge's family. Certainly her mother and father were quite sane, but I knew hardly anything of her grandparents. Maybe it didn't matter.

So Maria and Tommy came over the next night—a Tuesday—ostensibly for bridge, but actually to put Marge under quiet observation for a few hours. It started off tamely enough, but it developed into quite a remarkable evening.

We started playing bridge in the usual way, talking about the usual things—the Transylvania question, and Manchuria, and wasn't it shame about A.I.—but I could see that Maria and Tommy were watching Marge closely as if they had her in the hospital. They watched the co-ordination of her hands, they watched her eyes, and they dropped deft little, seemingly unrelated, questions into the stream of our conversation. And Marge, I do believe, appeared completely normal for the first hour or so, until she suddenly put down her cards and exclaimed, "I must have a dill pickle!"

"What's that?" Tommy asked.

"I must have a dill pickle!" Marge repeated. "If I don't have a dill pickle I shall go mad. Stephen, go to the delicatessen at once and get some dill pickles!"

"But, Marge," I protested, "that's absurd. We can't break up the game just because you have a sudden yen for a dill pickle!"

"Stephen, you hate me, don't you? But I must have a pickle."

"I think," Maria interrupted quietly, "that you had better go get a pickle, Stephen."

So I trotted around to the delicatessen and bought some dill pickles. "Don't slice them," Marge ordered when I got back. "I want them whole." I expected her to devour them whole, on the spot, but she bit into one, nibbled at a small piece of it, and then shoved them aside.

"Is that all you want?" I asked, indignant at all the trouble for one puny bit of pickle.

"That's all," she said. "Whose deal?"

I looked at Maria and Tommy. Obviously they were puzzled. Perhaps startled is a better word. Particularly Maria. "Darling," she asked Marge in a soothing voice, "do you often get a sudden hankering for a certain kind of food, like that? So you feel you must have it, absolutely must?"

"She certainly does," I said, "at the oddest hours."

"Shut up!" Marge told me. "Shut up! Haven't I any privacy in my own house?"

Tommy didn't say anything. He began to deal the cards. Maria kept her eyes on Marge, a queer, puzzled expression—you might call it compassion—shining out of her small dark face.

And then, in perhaps thirty minutes, Marge got up from the table, and slipped on her coat, and said, "You people will excuse me for a few minutes, won't you?"

"Where are you going?" I said. "Marge, we've got company. We're playing bridge."

"No, Stephen, I'll go myself," Marge said. "I don't want to bother you. It's so much trouble for you to go out and get something for me."

"Now, Marge," I said, "just tell me what you want and I'll get it." I found that I was afraid if she went out she would not come back. I recalled all the stories I'd written in my life about wives who got up from the bridge table, or left a cocktail party, and turned up at Bayonne, N. J., or Birmingham, ten days later with a beautiful and impenetrable amnesia.

"I was just going out and get some lemons," Marge said. "I've got a frightful craving for lemons."

"Aren't there some in the refrigerator?" I said.

"No, I'm afraid I ate them all," Marge said. "For days I've been devouring lemons. Dozens of them."

Maria said, as if she was repeating a witch's incantation, "Pickles and lemons, lemons and pickles." She touched Marge's arm and said, "Dear, I want to see you alone for a moment, in the bedroom."

"But my lemons," Marge said.

They went into the bedroom together. "What do you think of that performance?" I asked Tommy. I was shocked, but at the same time I was glad it had happened, because it gave Maria and Tommy such a perfect insight into the strange things that had been going on in the Chez Smith.

Tommy hunched his enormous shoulders and let his chin sink on his chest. "There's something in the back of my mind," he said.

"Don't you agree," I said, "that there is something wrong, mentally? These wild whims for food—and the jealousy. Of course you won't get a chance to see her when she starts accusing me, because she won't do it until you're gone. But it's really pathetic."

Tommy shook his head. "She's not crazy," he said. "She's emotionally disturbed, but she's not crazy. There's something pushing against her subconscious that gives us these symptoms. Brought into the open, they'd probably disappear. I just can't imagine what it would be, unless——"

"Unless what——"

"Skip it," Tommy said brusquely, and then Maria poked her head out of the bedroom door, and said would Tommy please come in for a moment. She sounded excited. Tommy went into the bedroom, and shut the door behind him, and my imagination began to play a rhythm of fear and apprehension inside my head.

Now you could see, I told myself, that it was serious. Maria taking Marge into the bedroom, like that, showed that she suspected something. And calling Tommy into consultation showed that she wanted him to confirm it. Once I thought I heard a sound like a frightened squeal. They remained in the bedroom for what seemed an unreasonably long time, although probably it was no more than fifteen minutes, and by the time they came out I was pacing the floor, a drink in my hand, and my hand was shaking.

I began, definitely, to hear noises from the bedroom. It sounded like Marge's laughter, but it was probably groans. Then they all came out, in a silent, tense little line, like the first three coming out of the jury room. Maria was first, Tommy second, and Marge last. If I remember correctly, they were all crying, or laughing, or both.

They walked over to me and Tommy took me by the shoulders and said, "Unless we are both mistaken, and we are both willing to stake our reputation on it, Marge is going to have a baby!"

I remembered staring down at the shattered glass that I had held in my hand, and the pool of soda bubbling around it. I found that Tommy was holding me up. "Stephen!" Marge said. "Stephen, what's the matter?"

"He's out on his feet," Tommy said. "He'll be all right in a second. Bring him another drink."

I drank it, and I looked at all of their faces and I could see that they weren't joking. For a long time all I could say was, "Impossible!" and then I sat down and began to think.

I thought very rapidly, and asked how long Marge had been pregnant, and Maria said about two months—probably a little longer—and I ticked the months off on my fingers, backwards, and arrived at Marge in Washington—with Homer Adam. Marge said, "I know just what you're thinking, Stephen Decatur Smith, and it isn't so. You're a suspicious, dirty old man."

"Oh, my," I said, "if it wasn't Homer, then who was it?"

"Him!" she said. She put her arms around Tommy's neck and kissed him on the mouth.

"Oh, no, it wasn't him," I said. "He's in exactly the same shape I'm in. You can't fool me, Marge. It was Homer. I can't say that I blame you. If you really want a baby, that was the only reliable way to have one."

"Oh, you darn fool," said Marge. "You don't understand at all, do you?"

"Naturally, I don't understand. What husband ever does understand?"

"Shall I explain?" Tommy asked.

"No, I'll tell him," Marge said, "although I really shouldn't. I really should let him think it was Homer."

"Go ahead," I said. "From now on I can take anything."

"It was Tommy's tonic—that seaweed stuff. It worked."

"Ha-ha. Ho-ho," I laughed. "I didn't take any!"

"Oh, yes, you did," Marge said. "You took a whole bottle. Do you remember that day in Washington you felt so bad? That day I spiked all your drinks, and the next morning I poured the rest of it into your coffee."

"My gosh," Tommy interrupted. "You were only supposed to give him forty drops a day. That's powerful stuff!"

"I know," Marge said, "but I wasn't going to be in Washington long, and so I gave him the whole bottle."

I felt affronted and outraged, as anyone does who discovers that somebody has been tampering with their food or drink. "You might have killed me," I said. "From now on I suppose I'll have to have a taster in this house."

Maria looked at me, almost in wonder. "But she didn't kill you," she said, "and you're going to be a father!"

Gradually, very gradually, for the mind cannot absorb so much at once, the full import and meaning of what had happened began to penetrate. For no good reason I began to shake Tommy's hand. "Congratulations," I told him. "You did it!"

He didn't seem to be listening. He said, as if talking to himself, "I wonder whether it was giving him the whole bottle at once, or whether it was mixing it with the rye, or whether it was mixing it with the coffee. I wonder whether it wasn't a freak, a phenomenon that won't be repeated. I wonder whether it wouldn't have happened spontaneously anyway. I wonder whether any of the guys at the hospital—"

"You can start figuring all that out tomorrow," Maria told him. "Right now, it's just wonderful."

Marge asked me whether I wasn't going to kiss her, and I kissed her for such a long time that Maria and Tommy stood by, fascinated, and watched, and Marge said she supposed she had been acting like a fool for a month or two, but she couldn't help it and now that she knew what was the matter I didn't have to worry any more.

"I ought to call the office," I said, "and give them a flash."

"I wouldn't—not yet," Maria warned. "Both Tommy and I are absolutely certain, and yet there's always that infinitesimal possibility of a mistake. We'll have a rabbit test made tomorrow, and then you can write your story." That sounded reasonable.

I do not remember much about the rest of that evening. But just before Maria left she asked Tommy, as if it were a matter of no importance, whether he himself had been taking the seaweed stuff, and Tommy said yes, of course, and as she tucked a hand under his elbow she said, "Tommy, I think we ought to get married, right away. I'm a little worried."

CHAPTER 16

I suppose the rest is history, rather than a personal narrative.

The positive reports on the rabbit test came through Wednesday night, and I called J.C. Pogey and said I had a flash, and he said it was about time that somebody produced a flash, because the world was rotting, and for the first time in his life he was getting bored with his job. I said that from now on he wouldn't be bored, because the flash was that I was going to have a baby.

"*You* are going to have a baby," said J.C. "If that happens I quit."

"Well, Marge is," I said.

"Whose?" he demanded sharply, no doubt thinking the same thing that I had thought when I first heard the news.

"Mine," I told him, and I told him how.

J.C. Pogey is a great newspaperman. He immediately foresaw all the possibilities that Tommy Thompson had foreseen—principally that it was just an isolated accident. He said, "We're not going overboard on this story. We'll just present it factually as it has happened thus far. We will not speculate."

But of course the world went quite mad, in spite of J.C. Pogey.

It turned out that the world was justified. Tommy Thompson discovered that his seaweed tonic, given in a dose not quite lethal and without the aid of alcohol or caffeine, jolted the paralyzed male germ into activity. In hardly any time all the internes at Polyclinic, and all Tommy's friends, were potent and careful.

The government immediately took over all production, and Phelps-Smythe, now a general, was entrusted with security. This was a most important post, because there was no doubt that the Russians were trying to steal the secret. They actually admitted it themselves.

There are plans, not entirely approved, for making Thompson's tonic available to every male in all the world, even the Outer Mongolians. But as things stand now the program is moving along like a boxcar with flat wheels being jostled into a siding.

All these plans have not been put into effect, because of the complications. At first the Thompson tonic was placed in the hands of N.R.C., but later N.R.P. was revived, combining all the best men of both organizations, under Abel Pumphrey.

While matters are not proceeding with great speed, it is quite understandable. After all the domestic issues are ironed out, there is the foreign problem. There is a group that believes that the UN should handle a good deal of it. But the Administration has decided that it is of much too vital importance for the UN. Being a young organization, perhaps the UN can handle things like the Transylvania boundary dispute, but certainly should not be entrusted with the secret of Thompson's tonic. All the commentators agree that Thompson's tonic is dynamite.

The Frame has abandoned her screen career, and is racing around the country presenting, in lectures, her proposals for founding a perfect race.

Homer Adam has resumed commuting to New York from Tarrytown. Suddenly he has become no more famous than Wrong Way Corrigan, Jess Willard, or Papa Dionne. Poor Homer is indeed a has-been, for he sterilized himself so thoroughly that not even Thompson's tonic can help him. This, he does not seem to mind.

It was eighteen months after our twins were born that J.C. Pogey made his last visit to us. It was the same day that Turkey announced it would fight if Russia tried to take the Straits; the Atlantic fleet set out for maneuvers near Iceland; Britain announced it was backing up the fortifications of Gibraltar; and France announced her expansion of bases in North Africa. It was just an ordinary day.

J.C. watched the twins playing in the play pen. Little Abel (I don't know why Marge insisted on naming him after Abel Pumphrey) was sitting down, playing with his blocks, and minding his own business. Little Stephen had found a tack hammer somewhere, and with it in his hand he was advancing on Abel as if to scalp him.

J.C. watched, fascinated, and he said, "This is where I came in," and left. We never saw him again.

ABOUT THE AUTHOR

PAT FRANK (1908–1964) is the author of the classic postapocalyptic novel *Alas, Babylon*, as well as the Cold War thriller *Forbidden Area*. Before becoming an author, Frank worked as a journalist and also as a propagandist for the government. He is one of the first and most influential science fiction writers to deal with the consequences of atomic warfare.

ALSO BY PAT FRANK

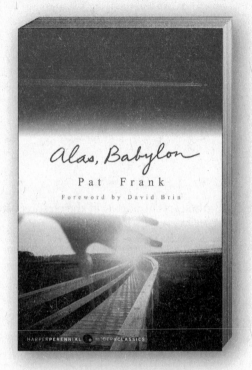

ALAS, BABYLON
A Novel

Available in Paperback and eBook

This true modern masterpiece is built around the two fateful words that make up the title and herald the end—"Alas, Babylon." When a nuclear holocaust ravages the United States, a thousand years of civilization are stripped away overnight, and tens of millions of people are killed instantly. But for one small town in Florida, miraculously spared, the struggle is just beginning, as men and women of all backgrounds join together to confront the darkness. Will Patton's narration paints this classic tale as an ominous picture of the terrible possibilities of the nuclear age.